Haters and Chasers

Kimberly Bibbs

In loving memory of my mother, Marian Larry Bibbs

Printed in the United States of America

ISBN 978-0-9762607-2-1

Dree Publishing
Houston, TX

www.kimberlybibbs.com

.

Acknowledgements

God. Thank You! This has truly been a journey. I thank You for the long walk to get to where You ordered me to go.

To my children, Kristyn, Stephanie, Derek, and Adrienne thank you for believing I could do this.

To my mom, who is an Angel now, and my dad for always reading to me when I was a child.

To my grandmother who showed unconditional love to everyone.

To my all night writers, Sheretta Edwards, Faynetta Lavergne Burrle, and Nakia Laushaul, thanks for the encouragement.

Thanks to my editor, Michelle Chester. You were so patient with me. Thanks for all of your hard work and advice.

Chapter 1

Justin sat on the edge of the bed staring into space. A week had gone by since Blair last called him and he hadn't answered his phone. Now Blair would not answer his phone calls at all. He had not talked to her the whole week. The longest he had gone without any communication from her was four days. After that time, his lies made sense to her and he knew it. Words weren't going to work for him any longer. Blair was becoming suspicious. But since she has never caught him in the act of cheating, he somehow felt safe. Blair had accused Justin of cheating on a couple of occasions, but his smooth talking, confident attitude got him out of many situations time and time again. He was hoping this time wouldn't be any different.

"She is going to believe me this time," he kept saying to himself. "I always know what to say and do to please her. Blair will never leave me." Justin was weak from thinking along with everything else he had just done with Arlene, his companion for the last couple of days.

He was trying to come up with a lie he had never used before. Justin looked down at his feet as he tapped them while trying to come up with something to say. He tried to stand up, but his body felt heavy like he was weighted down with some sort of object. The burden of lying was starting to be too heavy for him. But he didn't care. There were so many that he had buried in his memory, ready for retrieval at a moment's notice. He knew he had to always sound convincing because he never considered being faithful and was never afraid of being caught cheating. He was confident that his lies sounded like the truth. The only thing Justin feared was losing his ability to lie and get away with it. He really did love Blair, but his head kept telling him that being with only one woman for the rest of his life would not satisfy his appetite. *Giving away your heart can make you weak*, he thought.

Justin felt that the more money a man has, the more of a man he is. He was proud of his narcissistic behavior and how he treated women like objects. They were to be paraded around, have no opinion or say so in anything, especially if he was going to be associated with them in any way. Blair had a job, but once they got married, Justin would see to it that she terminated her employment and stayed home and went wherever or did whatever he wanted her to do at his command. He knew that would be a tough task. Blair was an independent woman when it came to taking care of herself and she let him know it.

Justin didn't know if he was this way because of his father. If so, he could blame it on his DNA. He grew up watching his father rule his mother with an iron clad law that she dared not break. *Whatever I say do, you just do it*, he remembered his father saying. *Don't ask me any questions about anything. You just be glad you have a roof over your head, a vehicle to drive, food to eat, clothes to wear, and money to buy whatever you want.* He remembered how his mother never asked his father anything. She didn't need to. As long as she had access to the bank account, no matter how hurt she was because of his father's infidelities, she would try to find comfort in spending as much money as she could. His mother always did as his father said and never once asked him where he had been or what he was doing.

But as many times as he had tried that tactic with Blair, it never worked. She badgered him and barraged him with questions. Sometimes asking them so fast and rephrasing some of the same questions that she almost tripped him up a couple of times. He had to become better at lying, because Blair wasn't the kind of woman that he could make shut up. Sometimes Blair unnerved him. He knew she had no fear of him. She said whatever she wanted to him and did whatever she wanted to do. He wasn't sure how far he could push Blair before she unexpectedly unleashed her wrath on him. Even though he didn't have a wife, he didn't want to end up like his father, who was shot dead by his mistress who got tired of him getting up in the middle of the night to go home.

Justin felt he had hit the jackpot with Blair. She was the type of woman he wanted to spend the rest of his life with—when he was ready. Blair was smart, poised, but her hot-assed temper was something he wished she didn't have. He knew Blair was a good woman, but she just wouldn't do what he told her to do. He knew he had to break her before they got married and make sure she knew his word was law. He wanted to get up and call her again, but couldn't do it at the moment.

"What's wrong with you?" Arlene stood in the bedroom doorway with her arms on each side of the door-frame drawing attention to her shapely form. Her hair was in perfect style. Her hands were well manicured and feet pedicured with matching strawberry red nail polish. The body was tight and she used it to get whatever she wanted when she wanted it. Her face was never without makeup. She kept herself that way from sun-up to sun-down to get a man and to keep him. Image is everything is her motto. She truly lived by those words and was going to do everything and anything to get this man. Even though she didn't want or love him, she was determined to get him anyway. Arlene wasn't looking to love anyone or have him love her. Just one man with a lot going on was enough for her. With enough money, she could pretend to love. She was looking to get a husband. Justin would do just fine. She was going to chase him until he was caught.

"Nothing," he said startled. Justin was glad that his thoughts could not be heard. His mind was still on Blair as he watched Arlene move from the doorway. Arlene was living the glamorous life. He hadn't shelled out any money on her yet. They had not been sleeping together that long. The lavish lifestyle she lived made him wonder for a fleeting moment how she maintained that lifestyle.

Arlene sashayed across the room to her bed leaving deep foot impressions in her plush white carpet. "You looked like you were so far away," she said. "Cheer up, sweetie. I don't like it when you look like that."

Justin took in a deep breath and exhaled loudly. "I'm still here, have been for days. I guess my employees think I've abandoned them." Justin looked at his watch. It was 1:15 p.m. He decided to take one more day off and go in tomorrow.

"Your body is here, but where's your mind?" Arlene asked. She seductively ran her hands through her hair, and then slid the index finger of her right hand horizontally across her lips and stood near the edge of the bed looking at him.

Justin stared back and didn't answer her question. *What are you thinking? I bet you have a plan to get as much money out of me as you can.*

Arlene waited for an answer, but got no response. "It can't be on work. You already said your staff had everything under control." Arlene climbed on the bed and put her chest against Justin's back. She wrapped her arms around his shoulders while blowing her warm breath in his ear.

Even though Justin enjoyed Arlene's warm breath gently moving across his right ear, his mind was still on Blair. He cut his thinking short and responded to Arlene. "Yeah, even though I have competent people running my construction company, I still have to show my face from time to time or my money will probably start walking out the door."

Arlene held him tighter. "It must be nice to have more money than you could spend in a lifetime." Arlene let out a sigh. "I bet you've traveled to a lot of places, bought a lot of things, and have no worries at all." She stroked his hair with her hand and then embraced him tighter.

Justin removed himself from her grip and looked around her bedroom. It was beautifully and expensively decorated. "It looks like money comes easy to you." He knew the white plush carpet she had in her bedroom was really expensive, especially to maintain. She was definitely high maintenance. He tried not to let Arlene see the distracted look that was on his face. He knew Blair was going to try to beat his ass when she saw him. She wasn't as sweet as everyone thought she was. *There really is a thin line between love and hate,* he thought. He wanted Blair to be like the rest of the women he had control of. He didn't know how much longer Blair would put up with him. After every encounter with her, he noticed that she became more distant. He didn't know if he was losing his touch when it came to controlling women or if Blair was the woman who was bold enough to stand up to him. But if she was going to be with him, she was going to have to conform.

Arlene rubbed her right hand across Justin's back and embraced him again. "What makes you think money comes easy to me?" Arlene released her grip and started fidgeting with her ring. "You must think that money just falls in my lap," she said sharply as she tried to get his attention with her raised voice. She put her arms around him again.

Justin came out of his thinking mode. "You have this beautiful house, nice car, and are always looking like you've stepped out of a fashion magazine. And yet I don't know what you do for a living. Come to think of it, I've been with you for a couple of days and you haven't said anything about a job or missing work." Justin noticed the expensive jewelry that was in her two foot jewelry box that was on the floor next to her dresser. The door was open and three expensive diamond necklaces were in full view. Her closet was huge. There was a wall with a built-in shoe rack. Justin guessed there were about 50 pairs of shoes lining the right side of the wall. Before he could focus his eyes to the left side of the closet while sitting on the bed, his attention was diverted when he felt Arlene loosening her grip.

Arlene tensed her shoulders, released Justin from her arms, and ran both of her hands through her hair. She got up and walked away from him and rested her arms on the back of the chair next to her closet. "You've only known me for two months. You know my name, address, and phone number, so why are you so curious about what I do?" Arlene was now gripping the back of the chair, digging her fingernails into it. After a few seconds, when her anger subsided, she loosened her grip from the chair, walked around to her bed, and propped herself on her left side with her back to Justin. Arlene didn't want Justin to see the nervous look on her face.

He turned and looked at her with a raised eyebrow. He saw that her back was facing him, and proceeded with his conversation anyway.

"You wanted to know what I did for a living. I think that was question number two when we first met. And I don't make a habit of asking a woman what she does for a living." Justin waited for her to turn around and face him. After a few moments he turned and focused his gaze on a picture on the night stand of Arlene posing in a V-neck black dress, leaning on a convertible silver Mercedes.

Arlene frowned and the furrowed lines on her forehead became more noticeable. She never turned to face Justin as she rubbed her hand across her forehead feeling for the lines that showed her irritation. She fixed her eyes on the wall. "You must have me mixed up with someone else, Justin. I never asked; you volunteered that information yourself when you handed me your business card. I was minding my own business at my girlfriend's party when you invited yourself over to where I was sitting."

Justin thought back to their first meeting and realized she was right. He had been so busy trying to impress people that he had rambled on about himself. "Sorry, you're right," he said. "But I only came over because you kept eyeing me up and down." Justin really wasn't concerned about how she supported herself, as long as she didn't start asking him for money. He wanted to be the one to offer if he chose to. "You know, just forget the whole thing. It doesn't matter. I see you can take care of yourself and it's no concern of mine of how you do it." He got up to go to the bathroom. He turned around as Arlene was moving to the other side of the bed. "You're not a prostitute, are you?" Justin chuckled out loud.

"What?" she asked stunned. Arlene's insides heated up. She was trying to control her anger. "Do you think I'm a prostitute?" Arlene rose up and was now in the bed with her knees under her. She watched Justin as he got up and walked over to the dresser. Her breathing became intense and her eyes started to water. She was insulted and humiliated. "A prostitute!"

Justin had a smirk on his face as he turned his back to her. He was only kidding. "Do I need to take my wallet in the bathroom with me?" Justin playfully picked up his wallet, pretended to count his money, and threw it back on the dresser. "Yeah, a prostitute is what I said," he joked. Justin felt his body become heavy again. It wasn't from the burden of lying he felt earlier. He felt like something was about to happen.

Arlene jumped from the bed onto Justin's back. "You must think I'm some woman off the street!" She held on tight as Justin swirled around and landed on top of her as they both fell on the bed. Justin had her by both wrists as he tried to slow her struggling.

"Okay, Arlene. Have you lost your damned mind?" Justin yelled. "Can't you take a joke? It was a damn joke, okay?" He was still on top of her trying to control her erratic hands from trying to land a punch on any part of his body. Arlene managed to get from under him with her hands swatting at the air. Justin pushed her back down and was on top of her again, trying to get her under control.

"So I'm a slut, huh?" she screamed as she landed on the bed. She was breathing short, fast breaths while struggling to get up from under

Justin again. "Let go of me!" She was panting. The left strap of her nightgown broke loose. "Get off of me!" Arlene got up and caught her loose night gown before it fell from her shoulder to reveal her left breast. She tried to push him off of her with her free hand, but Justin still had her by her wrist.

Justin was caught off guard by Arlene's reaction. "What's wrong with you? I was just kidding." His face turned to the right from Arlene's push. "Come on Arlene, stop it now," he shouted. "I was just playing with you. I don't think you're a slut." She was behaving like a mad woman. He wanted to tell her to shut the hell up and go sit down somewhere, but he realized that she had home field advantage. He was in her home so he knew he had to control himself. He didn't know what she had hidden in her room. He was afraid that she had easy access to a weapon to fend him off and then claim self-defense or worse have a hidden camera somewhere to prove that he attacked her if things got out of control. He decided to remain as composed as he could; otherwise he probably would have pinned her against the wall and dared her to move or say anything else to him.

Arlene finally stopped struggling as Justin freed her other hand. Her gown slipped from her left shoulder as she jerked her arm away from Justin. "What have you heard about me?" she asked. "I'm no prostitute or any man's slut." She sat up on the bed and pulled her nightgown up to cover her exposed breast and brushed her hair out of her face.

"Nothing," Justin said. "Nothing," he said again with force. Justin watched her as she jumped from the bed, pulled her hair back, and tucked it behind her ears. She held her gown up and walked to her dresser. She opened the drawer and took out a red short nightie. She let the other one fall to the floor. As she stepped out of it, Justin noticed the intense look on her face. His eyes followed her as she moved across the room. He wanted to make sure she didn't surprise him again with any sudden moves. *This woman is crazy*, he thought. Justin was breathing hard as he sat back down on the bed. Trying to control Arlene's movements was almost like fighting her to the death. "Damn," he said as he slowed his breathing.

Arlene took in a deep breath and quickly blew it out. She did it four more times. On the fifth breath, she was able to speak. "Yes, men buy me things and pay bills for me, but that doesn't mean I'm a prostitute." Arlene regained her composure, and after sitting on the edge of the bed for a few seconds, she got up and walked nervously over to her dresser to get a cigarette. "Is that what you think of me?" Arlene picked up the pack and tapped three times until a cigarette dispensed from the pack. She lit it, took three puffs, and smashed it in the ashtray on her dresser.

What the hell is wrong with her? Justin was still trying to slow his breathing. "I'm not apologizing for what I said." He moved closer to the edge of the bed, facing the dresser mirror. "I don't think you are a prostitute, but you're probably just a step above it."

Arlene wiped the crocodile tears from her eyes. "A step above a prostitute. What's that supposed to mean?"

"An expensive call girl. Wouldn't that be better than a prostitute?"

He saw Arlene wipe a tear from her eye. He didn't know if Arlene was putting on an act. *Every woman I come in to contact with is a damn psycho*. Justin put his face in his hands. *I've got to be more careful of who I spend the night with. What is wrong with me? I need to get it and get out the same damn night.* He knew his craving for female attention kept him wired and made him feel as if he were on top of the world. Justin removed his face from his hands. While sitting on the edge of the bed, he noticed that Arlene was too quiet after her tantrum she had just thrown. He was now afraid to go into the bathroom to take a shower. "Are you okay?" he asked as if he cared.

"Why do you care? I'm one step from being a prostitute as you put it," she snapped back. "I'm fine. I thought you were going to take a shower."

"I'm going now." Justin got up and walked slowly to the bathroom. Once he was in the shower, he quickly lathered and rinsed twice. He didn't bother to close the shower door. He didn't want Arlene sneaking into the bathroom ready to attack. When he finished, he quickly dressed. It was time to face Blair, again.

*****

The drive to Blair's house seemed like an eternity. Justin took the long route, giving him time to get enough nerve to face her. Making sure his rehearsed lines were new, he said them out loud. He knew his apology had to sound sincere and he needed to appear remorseful. The same old lines would not work on Blair this time. He thought about stopping by the Galleria to pick up a gift for her, but decided against it. Gifts didn't work with Blair anymore. So he passed up the Westheimer exit and continued on, finally arriving at Blair's home fifteen minutes later.

Chapter 2

Blair was past furious; she was livid. When Justin was near her home, he called and told her he would be there in three minutes. She met him at the door as he used his key to enter her home. "So where have you been for the last week?" Blair was poking Justin in the chest, trying to hold back the tears. Before he could answer, she blurted, "I'm tired of the lies, Justin." She looked for some sign of remorse on Justin's face. All she could see was the same old lying look that she had become accustomed to. She turned and walked to her sofa as Justin followed behind her with his hands in his pocket and a smirk on his face.

"Now, why do I have to be lying? You're always thinking that I'm lying to you. I haven't lied about anything. I tried to call you back and you didn't answer." Justin wished Blair would slow down with the questions because he couldn't think that fast. He remained composed while answering Blair's question, but he couldn't control his sweating.

Blair turned around quickly, walked away from the sofa, and stood in front of Justin. "Why are you sweating Justin, huh? Look at you. Face all wet," Blair yelled.

Justin wanted to pull his hands out of his pockets to wipe his face, but he kept his clenched hands hidden. He always became agitated when women questioned him about what he did. His clenched hands were a natural reaction. But sweating, that was something that he never did when it came to defending himself against a woman. He wondered why this time was different. He couldn't quite predict what was going to happen with this encounter. Blair was in rare form.

"You didn't put forth an effort to answer any of my calls this past week," Blair yelled.

"At least I tried to call you back." Justin's voice was loud and stern. "Why didn't you answer the phone when I called you?" Justin asked.

"Answer the phone for what, Justin? I was too angry to talk to you because I already knew you had your lies together." Blair took short, quick steps from one end of the room to the other end and repeated her actions a couple of times before she could continue interrogating Justin. "Don't come in here questioning me, you lying bastard. What in the hell is wrong with you?"

"Why do I have to be a lying bastard?" he asked. He relaxed his jaw as he stared straight ahead not looking at Blair. Justin let out a slight huff and casually turned to go into the kitchen to get himself a bottle of water while Blair was still talking. He wasn't worried or cared about what she was saying. He opened the refrigerator and looked around to see what was there. He saw a couple of cans of Coke, a package of cheese, and yogurt. He decided to go with the water. He grabbed the bottle, opened it, and took two quick swallows. He put the top back on the half-empty bottle and sat it on the counter. As he was walking back to the living room, he stopped when he noticed Blair's cell phone on the other end of the counter. He picked it up and didn't care if Blair walked in and saw him. He scrolled through the list of called numbers and smiled when he didn't see any other male numbers besides his in it. He laid it back down on the counter and slowly walked back into the living room with his hands in his pocket, face relaxed, and confident that whatever else he told Blair, she would believe it. She was still talking when he walked back in.

Blair met Justin at the entrance and continued with her rant. Justin's brief disappearance didn't silence her at all. "I called you on Friday, three times," she said, holding up three fingers as she held them close to his face. "I called you once on your home phone, I called you on your cell and," she said with emphasis while tears were rolling down her face, "I called your office. Why didn't you answer any of your phones?" Blair quickly backed away from Justin to keep herself from crying harder than she already was. She was torn between telling him it was over or listening to what lie he was going to tell this time.

Justin overlooked Blair's tears. They didn't upset him or tug at his heart strings. He just wanted the sobbing noise to go away. The sound of crying irritated him. The snorting and hesitation between sobs put a frown on his face, and he shook his head from side to side in disgust.

"I left my cell phone in the car and I guess I didn't hear my home phone ring when you tried to call me." Justin paused before giving an explanation about his office phone. He didn't see that one coming. He wished Blair would stop with the quick questions because he couldn't think fast enough to give a believable answer this time. "And, oh, you know I don't just sit around my desk all day. I do have to go out to my construction sites occasionally."

"I guess you took your time to get your cell phone out of your car or to check your home caller ID." Blair stopped pacing when she got to her end table near the window. She slammed her fist on the table, grabbed the junk mail that was there, and threw them across the room. She turned back around to face Justin and stared at him without saying a word. She wanted him to tell the truth for once, even though she knew it would make her want to crumple on the floor and cry until she couldn't cry anymore. She didn't want any more money, gifts, vacations, and certainly no more lies from him. She wanted to know that she wasn't overreacting or letting her imagination get the best of her. Sometimes she second guessed herself depending on what lie Justin told. She would think about it for a couple of days and realize that he had to be telling the truth. Justin wouldn't cheat on her she would tell herself. Then it would happen again. She looked at Justin as he stood there going on about why she doesn't trust him and how she should know that he would never cheat on her.

Blair's quietness led him to keep lying as he walked to her side of the living room. "I was busy all week with work, and then I slept most of the weekend."

As soon as those words left his mouth, she knew that he was busted. She knew he had to think of something else to say. Blair knew he only needed about five hours of sleep a night. Blair was quick. She picked up the heavy crystal clock that was on the table and threw it across the room. It missed Justin by inches. He ducked out of its way. "I'm supposed to be your woman, and you go a whole week without answering my phone calls." She quickly looked for another object to throw, but there was nothing else heavy enough to do any damage.

"What the hell!" Justin straightened up from his crouched position. "I'm tired of people jumping me and throwing shit at me. I don't know what else to tell you, Blair." Justin's heart was beating faster than normal, because he almost didn't see the clock coming at him. Even though he was getting tired of women attacking him, he continued with his lying. "Blair, calm down and don't throw another thing at me. I mean it."

Blair walked over to Justin. "So," she yelled, "who else has been throwing things at you?"

Justin pointed his finger at Blair. "What the hell are you talking about?" He took a deep breath and put his right hand across his chin for a second. He removed his hand and crossed his arms. He stared straight at Blair. "Let me tell you something, don't ever talk to me like I'm a little boy. If you won't respect me like the man I am, then I have no business being here with a disrespectful woman like you." Justin unfolded his arms. "And to answer your question," he said forcefully, "no one else throws things at me. You're the only one."

Blair moved so close to Justin's face that their noses almost touched. "Disrespectful!" She stared into his eyes. She wasn't scared of Justin. She knew he probably had other women scared of him, but all Justin did was bark orders and tell lies. "I'm being disrespectful because I say what I want to say to you." She waited for Justin to say something. She could tell he had his eyes fixated on something else. Their eyes were no longer on each other even though she was right there in his face. He was looking at the wall behind her. "So," she said, "out of all of your women, I'm the only one throwing things at you?"

Justin was scanning the room for more potential items that Blair might want to throw at him. "Damn it, Ar… Blair. You're the only woman in my life, period." Justin caught himself before Arlene's full name came out. But he wasn't sure if he was quick enough. He couldn't tell by Blair's reaction. She was already in her "out of control" mode.

Blair walked back over to the end table. She heard the first syllable out Justin's mouth before he corrected himself. She was too drained to address it. "You know, Justin, I'm tired. I'm really tired. I can't do this anymore."

Justin didn't bother to really look at Blair. Just being there should be enough for her. He had other things on his agenda for the day. He would pencil Blair in another time. He needed to go to the cleaners, get his car detailed, and work out at the gym for a couple of hours. "Blair, you need to stop being so insecure. It doesn't look good. It makes you look weak. And weakness is a quality I despise." He sighed. "Get it together, Blair."

"Get it together," she yelled. "I am together. You just can't handle me and that bothers you." She walked away from the table and back towards Justin. "I don't know what you want or what you're looking for and I'm tired of trying to figure it out. If you don't want me, just let me know." She was breathing hot breath on Justin's face as she quickly listed all of his indiscretions. She did so with her hands resting behind her back. She had clutched in her hand a letter opener that was on the table with the mail. She'd picked it up while Justin was distracted for a moment. "Do you still want me, Justin?"

Justin saw how angry Blair was, but he knew she didn't care that her anger showed. That was the part that bothered him. He wished they could conclude this argument because he was ready to go. This time took longer than usual to wear Blair down. He didn't like how she was looking at him. She was now too calm. He thought she was getting ready to let him off the hook with all of the questioning. "Blair?" he called. "Blair?" He waited for her to answer. She slowly approached him without saying a word.

Blair finally realized what the meaning of crimes of passion was. Her mind started to drift away. *Should I stab him one time to let him know I mean business, or just stab until I feel satisfied?* Blair thought about keeping Justin in a trance with her hot glaring stare. *All I have to do is slice his ass up,* she thought. She was starting to lose all sense of reality. Her adrenaline had her so pumped that she was on a high.

She kept her hand behind her back. Blair kept telling herself to put the letter opener down. *He is still staring me in the eyes. The bastard is trying to look serious. I don't believe this. He's good.* Blair started to become light-headed. *Why am I still in love with this man? Why can't I just let go and forget about him? I'll be all right in time. Time.* Blair started thinking about all of the time she had invested in their relationship. When she got to month nine, her anger intensified. She knew she had put too much into this relationship to just tell Justin it was over and let him walk away. She knew Justin could get another woman as soon as his foot hit the driveway. *I wonder what he's telling the other women about me. That I'm not good in bed, I'm just a friend, I'm the one hanging on to him. Are they laughing behind my back? Are they helping him to think of lies to tell me when he is out with them?* Blair was mad, mad, mad. But not mad enough to kill Justin. She turned around making sure Justin saw the letter opener in her hand. She turned back around and calmly laid it back on the table.

Justin was about to offer an explanation before he saw the letter opener. "What the hell were you going to do with that?" he asked, referring to the potential weapon Blair once had in her hand. He waited for Blair to answer him.

"Do with what? This?" she asked sarcastically, pointing to the letter opener. "I don't know. You tell me. What did you think I was going to do with it?" She picked it up again and tapped the pointed end on the table a couple of times before putting it back down.

"Can you just step away from the table? You're making me nervous." Justin held out his arms to her. "Come here, baby. You know I love you, and you're the one I want to be with."

Blair stayed where she was and took a couple of slow breaths to calm herself down. *What was I thinking? I was about to kill him. Oooh, by the grace of God.* Blair quickly inhaled through her nose to keep it from running. It didn't work. She used the back of her hand to wipe the wetness from the top of her lip. "Well, I guess you didn't want me last week, because you were nowhere to be found." She turned away from him to hide the anger on her face. "Justin, I hate you," she cried. "I really hate you. Not only for what you're doing to me, but for thinking that I'm so senseless to believe everything you tell me." The little feelings she had for Justin were quickly fading. "Justin, I love you unconditionally. There is no reason for you to treat me the way you do." Blair was crying. "I've told you over and over again how I feel about you." She walked over to the window and leaned her head against the cool glass pane. She needed something to cool her warm, flushed face. "What am I doing wrong, Justin?" She took a deep breath to keep from hyperventilating. She hurt so deep inside but knew she needed to pull herself together.

Justin's heart was still beating fast. "I'm sorry," he said, waving his hands. "I was wrong for not calling, but you act like I was out doing something wrong."

Blair lifted her head and looked out the window, thinking about all the lies and all the women that Justin allowed to come between them. She didn't want to look at Justin. "You're not going to admit it. Why would you? I see that you don't give a damn about me. You're arrogant and selfish. You don't worry about my feelings or what I'm going through." Blair lifted the bottom of her pink spaghetti strapped tank top and wiped her face. "All I have ever wanted is someone to love and to be loved back. How can you keep leading me on like this if you know you can't make a commitment to me?"

"Blair, stop talking crazy. I do worry about you," Justin said. He glanced at his watch. This was taking longer than their normal routine and he was ready for this drama to end as quickly as possible.

"No, you don't Justin," Blair whispered. "No, you don't." She walked around and sat on the edge of her sofa after she caught a glimpse of Justin looking at his watch. "Is there somewhere you have to be?"

"Oh, so now I can't look at my watch without you questioning me?"

"You have a problem answering the question?"

"No, I don't, but let's get back to what we were talking about." Justin cleared his throat. "Okay, Blair, I'm going to be honest and tell you what I was doing over the weekend." Justin cleared his throat again, giving him time to think before he spoke. He had to be convincing.

Blair already knew what was coming. Justin's mouth was full of lies. She didn't know what he was about to say, but she knew it wouldn't be the truth.

"I wanted to surprise you. I was out looking for rings," he blurted out.

Blair turned and looked at him with anger in her eyes. "Stop it, Justin. I don't want to hear anything about rings, marriage, or any other lies that come out of your mouth." She closed her eyes for a couple of seconds, and then opened them again. She wanted to tell him to stop right there because she knew he was lying. Justin thought money and gifts were the cure all for all women, but Blair wasn't having it. She listened to him go on and on. "Okay, Justin. If that's your story, fine. I don't believe it."

"See, when I try and tell you the truth, you don't want to believe me, that's why I don't tell you everything I do. I hate arguing. That's all we do because you don't believe anything I say or do. You're always thinking I'm lying to you. Damn girl, when are you going to stop all of this? We'll never get along if you don't stop accusing me of things that I'm not doing."

Blair held her hand up. "Okay, Justin, I've heard enough." She wished he would leave before her murderous intentions resurfaced.

Justin walked towards Blair with his arms flaring everywhere. "I know you don't believe me. Everything is all on me. What about that time when I called your house at 10:30 at night three months ago and you didn't answer the phone?"

"Justin, that was three months ago. Why are you bringing that up? I was here. I was just getting out of the shower and I called you back and you didn't answer." Blair rubbed her temples to ease the tension on the side of her head.

"How do I know you called me back? I didn't see your number on my phone." He knew that was the night he was at his place with a woman he'd met at a business luncheon. Justin had turned his cell phone off and unplugged the one in his home after Blair didn't answer. "You're always trying to say what I do and don't do. How do I know you were really at home?" Justin was desperately trying to get the focus off of him.

"I told you I was. Who would I be out with? Has anyone ever come back and told you they saw me out with another man?" Blair watched Justin look up in the air and then focus his eyes back on her.

"If you were at your home with another man, no one would see you." Justin crossed his arms across his chest.

"Oh, but you have been seen with plenty of women." Blair walked back to the table where the letter opener was. She almost reached out her hand to pick it up but stiffened her arms at her sides to make sure she didn't make any sudden, stupid moves. "But you told me not to believe anything that I didn't see. Since you haven't seen another man at my house, why would you think I had one over?" *He did it again.* Blair knew he did it again and she let him. He was a master at taking the focus off of himself and placing it on her. "Justin, we discussed that and dealt with it. Leave it alone. It has nothing to do with what we are talking about now."

Justin kept his distance. "Oh when it's on you, you don't want to discuss it. See how you women are."

"What do you mean by, you women? You are discussing this with me. Where do other women come in?" Blair asked.

"Don't try to change the subject, Blair." Justin walked to the sofa and sat down.

Blair walked over to where he was and stood in front of him. She swiped her hands across her face, but there were no more tears. She wanted to get Justin out of her house. “Okay Justin, I don’t want to talk about it. Just go.”

“So you don’t want to talk about what you do? Now, you’re telling me to go.” Justin stood up and tried to kiss her on the cheek. “Come on, let’s go in the bedroom.”

Blair pushed him away. “Go back to where you were last weekend. You’re getting nothing from me.”

“I haven’t been with anyone. There you go with your imagination. I’ve never cheated on you, Blair.”

Blair managed to keep her cool after that statement. She knew a lot more than what Justin thought she did, but she kept in all inside. *Your day is coming.* The look in her eyes was pure hatred. She knew it wouldn’t do any good to question Justin about anything. He was a master liar. “Okay, okay, just go. I’ll call you when I’m ready to see you.” She pushed Justin toward the door. She couldn’t stand the sight of him anymore.

Justin gave Blair a kiss. “Okay, babe. Call me tonight when you’ve calmed down.” He calmly walked to the front door unaware that Blair was right behind him. He opened the door, exited, and closed it without looking back.

Blair looked out the door window and watched Justin as he walked out onto her porch and stopped to take something out of his pocket.

She couldn't tell what it was. She thought maybe it was his wallet or the so-called ring he said he purchased, the one he never produced during their argument. He had his back toward the window. "What is he doing?" she whispered. Finally, Justin's movements gave way to what he was doing. "Oh, so you are going to stand on my front porch and check your damn cell phone," she yelled as she turned off the porch light. "Don't use my light to do your dirty work! You don't even have the decency to get out of my sight before you get your cell out."

"Damn," Justin whispered. He quickly put his phone back in his pocket and walked to the driveway. He stood near his car. He knew Blair was still mad, but she'd be okay in a couple of days. He had a look of victory on his face. *I talked my way out of this one again. I will give her a couple of days to cool off,* he thought. Justin got in his pearl white Jaguar and made his way to whatever woman was available for the night because he knew Blair wouldn't be calling him for the next couple of days.

Blair was leaning on the front door. "Heartbreaker." She sobbed. She leaned harder against the door trying to regain her composure. "Why can't you just tell me that you don't want me?" The tears streamed quickly down her cheeks as she cried harder. After a couple of minutes she became tired of standing and she slowly slid to the floor and continued to cry until she couldn't cry anymore.

Chapter 3

Blair was giving her all on the treadmill. Running at a slow, steady pace for forty-five minutes left her drenched. She kept hitting the incline and decline button every two minutes, changing the pace for maximum effect. She almost lost her footing when she looked up and saw fine Eduardo coaching a woman on how to jump rope properly. He was one of the gym's top personal trainers. He was fierce with his training and she stayed away because she was scared of the tactics he used to get people through their workout. He strongly suggested that they keep up or else. Blair worked hard to maintain her athletic physique, but she didn't want to die trying. Three days a week she was at the gym. Today she was working out longer than usual. She didn't want to sit at home and brood and had to do something to keep from acting on the crazy thoughts that kept coming into her mind. She usually worked out in the evening, but it was early morning and she couldn't sleep.

Blair knew Justin admired how she kept her body in shape. He always told her to make sure she worked out at least three times a week to keep that gorgeous figure of hers. Letting her body go was not an option for her. But today, this exercise routine was all for her. She was so frustrated and didn't want to go into a self-pity state. There was so much anger built up in her that she almost put her fist through the wall in her hallway. But she had second thoughts when she realized that injuring her hand was not going to make her anger towards Justin go away.

Blair got off the treadmill, took her towel, and wiped her face and the back of her neck. She walked down the aisle towards the Stairmaster. All were taken. She decided to wait for a couple of minutes to see if anyone was almost done. She passed the time by looking through the glass window of a Zumba class. It was packed. There were people of all sizes and all levels of fitness in the class. She could barely hear the music from where she was standing. Whatever was playing was at a fast pace. Most of the class was on step, but there were a number of people who were slightly off step, some making up their own steps, and three others sitting against the wall out of breath. Blair watched for about three minutes, forgetting that she was waiting for a Stairmaster to become available. She was assessing the people who could not seem to keep up and saw about six people whom she concluded had no rhythm. The five who were making up their own steps probably didn't care if they were doing it right or not, they just wanted to be in Zumba class, and the three against the wall shouldn't have come at all.

She saw about fifteen more who may have been in the class for the first time, but had potential. She turned around to see an empty Stairmaster, but wasn't quick enough to get to it before someone beat her to it. She walked back to the empty treadmill she had left earlier, placed both feet on each, and started punching in numbers—weight, 135; incline, 4; speed, 4.5; time, 60 minutes. Blair was still mad!

*****

Hit him upstyle, in the wallet, in the head, whatever makes you feel good. Those thoughts would not leave Blair's mind. After her torturous workout at the gym, she decided to go on a shopping spree. She walked around and around in Carole's boutique picking up items that she didn't need or want. Her left arm was heavy from the weight of the clothes she had draped across it. Blair didn't bother to look at price, color, or style of the clothing that she grabbed off the racks.

Justin kept her life in a tailspin and her mind unfocused. She kept thinking about where he could be and with whom. Blair called him the night he left her house after she had calmed down from her hysterical, crying episode. She wanted her house key back. That's what she was going to tell him she was calling for and that she was done with him. But she was afraid if he had said the right words, she would succumb to his sweet words, forgive him, and let him keep the key. As usual, Justin didn't answer his home phone and she knew he had his cell phone turned off because it went straight to voicemail. The same cycle went on for the past three months. She had now become very tired and very angry. She knew it was time to move on. She didn't want to be with Justin on his terms.

All that Blair could think about now were ways to get back at Justin, to make him feel as bad as she had for the last year and a half. Blair didn't even notice the woman who accidentally bumped into her and apologized. She was in a daze. Her mind was flooded with questions about what it was that she was doing to make Justin do what he was doing.

Blair was crying on the inside, but at home the tears flowed effortlessly. She had gotten to the point where disappointment had gotten the best of her. She had once been strong, but she was now weak. Her spirit and self-worth were falling fast. Trying to make Justin happy consumed her. Her female coworkers had told her she was fighting a losing battle where Justin was concerned and she should try to use her energy for something else, because men come and men go. That's just the way it is. If Justin didn't want her, she wished he would just tell her so she can go on with her life. It was so hard for her to believe that Justin could lie to her and feel no remorse, shame, or guilt. Blair kept trying to figure out what she was doing to make Justin treat her the way he did.

She even cut out her overtime as an attorney in the Criminal Prosecutions Division with the Texas Attorney General's office so she could devote more time to working out to keep her velvety brown body in top condition. The boot camp workouts in addition to her gym time were torture, but she endured the workouts for the benefit of keeping Justin happy. Forty minutes of running, hundreds of push-ups, and squats had her so well-toned and burning calories at a high rate that she was able to eat whatever she wanted and not gain a pound.

She wore her shoulder length, light brown hair straight just the way Justin liked her to. That's how he said he liked it and that is how she kept it. She was a lady in public and whatever Justin wanted her to be in private. But now her thinking pattern had changed when it came to Justin. *To hell with him!*

The pictures she received in the mail five months ago, the message left on her answering machine four months ago, and the earring she found rolled in Justin's sheet in his hamper two weeks ago confirmed what she had long suspected. Those were tricks of the trade left by women who wanted Blair to know about them. The message she heard on her answering machine was the most damning and most hurtful of all. She knew for sure that she could never trust Justin again.

Justin's famous lines were etched in her brain. *How can you say that I'm cheating if you haven't seen me with anyone? And just because women call me doesn't mean I'm sleeping with them. Have you ever caught me sleeping with other women? I can be friends with women without sleeping with them.*

Justin was talented at flipping the script when he was about to become trapped in a lie. That was the tactic Blair unconsciously allowed him to use. It always worked, because it made her lose focus on what he was accused of doing. Their conversation always took a different turn and they would end up discussing every past argument they ever had. According to Justin, all of the arguments were her fault.

Once a month, like clockwork they got into an argument about something. Justin would be right on time with his prepared lines. He would bring up occasions when he called her house and she didn't answer the phone. This put Blair into a defensive mode, explaining to him for the umpteenth time where she was, which was most of the time at home, and she just didn't get to the phone before it stopped ringing.

Deep inside, Blair knew the real truth. She was not really mad at Justin anymore but upset at herself for taking so long to finally realize that no matter what kind of woman she was, if Justin was going to cheat, that's what he was going to do. There was nothing that she could do to change that. This had been going on for years and nothing could make him stop or even make him attempt to stop his cheating.

The thought of all the no good men she had come into contact with in the last ten years made her wonder who would teach the little boys to become real men. "God help them," she said under her breath. Blair stayed with Justin the longest because unlike the others, she really loved him.

She remembered the first time they met. They saw each other at the same time. Their eyes instantly locked together in a stare. As they walked toward each other, they both knew that moment would be the beginning of a relationship. There was no hesitation, no shyness, no forethought on either part about what will be said, who will speak first, or do I look all right. They both spoke to each other as if they had met long ago and had been reconnected. Blair remembered how he reached out his hand and asked her how she was doing. She caught his right hand in both of her hands as she softly shook it and replied that she was doing fine. “I’m Justin, Justin Vanderbilt,” he said.

“And I’m Blair Harris.” She remembered how she stared into his eyes, looked adoringly at his handsome face, and being bold enough to run her hands up his muscular arm as she continued to hold his hand with her other hand.

Justin clutched Blair’s hand tighter and led her to a corner of the conference room where there was less noise from the voices of the others who were networking with each other. “We’re not going to do the business card game, are we?” he asked. “I mean after we get the small talk out of the way, you’re not going to pull out a business card and tell me to call you if I need anything?”

“Well.” Blair coughed slightly to clear her throat. “Excuse me, sorry about that. But no we won’t. So just give me your phone number now and we can skip all the small talk.”

“Can I have your number, too?”

“Of course you can. And it will be the correct number, so don’t worry about me trying to give you a wrong number.” She smiled. “I’ll give you my home and cell numbers.”

“Are you going to answer when I call?”

“Maybe,” she answered quick and short. “There are times when I don’t feel like being bothered. I screen my calls occasionally.” She waited for Justin to respond to her statement. He didn’t. “I have an old school answering machine. So if you call, leave a message in case I’m not near the phone. If I hear your voice and I feel like talking, I'll pick up." She waited for Justin to say something. Again, he didn't. "Are you listening to me?"

He smiled. "I heard everything you said. You are up front and blunt."

"That I am, but in this case, I'm being truthful about who I am and to let you know that I don't and won't sit by the phone waiting for a man to call me." This time, Justin was ready to respond, but she interjected. "And don't come at me with you bet I have a lot of men and I pick and choose which days I want to see them." She folded her arms and smiled. "I don't operate that way."

"That's not what I was going to say."

"Yes it was," she shot back.

He laughed. "How did you know?"

"Because. I'm an attorney. I get paid to know."

Blair didn't want to think about how she met Justin anymore. She didn't know as much about Justin as she thought she did. His god-like personality didn't show up until their fifth date. She thought he would change. He didn't. She decided that as of today, his latest indiscretions would be the last things she would ever allow him to do to her. Blair was finished with him this time. She ran out of options and ultimatums. None of them worked. Like a fool, she knew she stayed with him too long. He would often tell her she was his number one, like that was some sort of high compliment. She didn't want to be number one; she wanted to be the only one. Her friends told her it wouldn't last and she tried her best to prove them wrong. Now Blair was tired.

She came back to her senses. A red pantsuit caught her eye. It was powerful. Blair figured since she didn't feel important, she could look the part in that power suit. She was trying to buy power, since she had been giving it away lately. Blair had often reset her boundary lines, hoping that Justin would not cross them.

Blair saw a gorgeous black dress. It was sexy. She took it off the rack and held it in front of her. *Perfect fit*. If she wanted to set the stage for a sexy night, that dress would warrant an encore performance. She felt she no longer had sex appeal and thought new clothes would make her desirable. Blair often wondered what Justin saw in other women that he did not see in her.

The three-inch heeled shoes with fake diamond trim caught her attention. They were expensive. She wanted to feel like she was worth something. Those shoes would make her feel as if she was walking on cloud nine. Blair took them out of the box, looped the straps through her fingers, and walked to the checkout counter.

Blair thought about how she would love to be all dressed up, looking sexy for a man who appreciated her. She imagined herself out on a date with a handsome man and running smack dab into Justin. The look on Justin's face would be priceless. Blair wanted to show him that other men desired her and that she didn't have to sit around waiting for him to grace her with his presence. She wanted to show him that she had found a man that loved and respected her. That wasn't about to happen because she didn't know any men like that.

Blair put everything on the counter without looking at the price of any of the items. She took out the charge card and handed it to the sales associate and wondered if she needed to go and add a little more damage to the account. Earlier in the day Blair had been fired up about buying things she really didn't want and making Justin pay for them. She came off of her high as soon as she handed the credit card to the sales lady. Justin gave her anything and everything she wanted, so she knew it wouldn't have mattered to him one bit that she was out spending his money, as long as she didn't question him about his whereabouts. Money was one thing Justin didn't worry about. What did worry and agitate him to the core were questions about how he lived his life. Other things came to her mind that would do far more damage, but Blair figured they weren't worth spending the rest of her life in jail for.

The Visa card in Blair's possession had Justin Vanderbilt's name on it, the boyfriend she was going to *get rid of* as soon as "approved" flashed across the screen. This was the only expensive boutique that she could go in and use Justin's card without any questions about the large amount of money charged to the card. They usually shopped together at Carole's Boutique, so Blair knew she was very well known and envied. She knew Justin loved the attention he received when he walked into the boutique with beautiful Blair on his arm. He wanted everyone to see what he had and that he could still do what he wanted to do and keep her, and she let him get away with it every time she was seen with him. Blair hated pretending not knowing about all of the women in Justin's life. She would smile and play along of how happy she was to be with him. There were times she felt like twisting his arm and yanking him out of the boutique from the watchful eyes of people who knew Justin was cheating. It was his fault the way people looked at her when they were together. They knew that she knew he was a cheater.

Approved flashed across the screen. *He's history,* she thought. Blair watched as Denise, the sales associate, neatly hung the dresses in the specialty garment bags with *Carole's Boutique* written in gold lettering. While waiting for her merchandise, she again thought back to when she first met Justin. She had to stop herself. No matter how many times she thought about it, the outcome would remain the same. Blair picked up her bags, took the charge card from Lita, the other sales associate, looked at it, and then decided she didn't want it anymore. She gave it back to her. "I won't need this anymore. When you see Justin, tell him I said thanks, and I hope he has a happy life."

As Blair walked out the door, it suddenly hit her that running up Justin's credit card wouldn't do a thing to him. She couldn't bleed him dry. He had way too much money. The high she felt when she walked into the boutique earlier had disappeared. She had an armful of bags with expensive clothing, shoes, and jewelry, but nowhere to go and nothing to do. "Damn you, Justin," she said under her breath. "You must think I'm a fool." She became weak and sick to her stomach. Her head started hurting. She was thinking about too many stressful things all at once. "I'm tired of Justin hurting me. I can't go on like this." The unthinkable came to her wounded heart as she walked out of the boutique.

Chapter 4

Lita looked at Denise, then at the card. "Are you thinking what I'm thinking?" Lita asked. She looked toward the door waiting for Blair to come and take the card back.

Denise looked at the card Lita had tightly clutched in her hand. "I don't know what you're thinking, but it's so sad that it took her this long to realize what kind of man she has. He's been seen around town, uptown, and out of town with a different woman every two weeks and all of them know about Blair." Denise watched as Blair walked out the door dangling her bags. She blew out the breath she temporarily held as she watched Blair take slow steps down the sidewalk until she was no longer in sight. She didn't expect to run into this kind of drama at her part-time job.

"Women on the side don't care about the women at home," Lita said.

Denise walked from behind the counter. "Well, it shouldn't have taken her almost three years to figure all this out. I heard that's how long they've been dating."

Lita looked at Blair's receipt copy. "And a measly fifty-five hundred dollars on his charge card isn't going to hurt him at all if she is trying to get back at him. But maybe she just needed new clothes." Lita placed the receipt copy in the register drawer. "She has lost weight in the last month, not a lot, but it is noticeable. He probably has her so stressed out that she can't bring herself to eat. I would've gotten rid of him a long time ago and found me someone else."

"Maybe she's just trying to get his attention," Denise said. "Do you remember two weeks ago when she was getting her hair done at Reece's Beauty Salon?"

"Yeah," Lita said. "Everyone that was there that day remembers how she went on and on about the no good women Justin had been out with."

"It was like she thought some of the women were there that day, like she was sending them a message," Denise said. "Come to think of it she did say she had something planned that would get his attention. I guess this mini-shopping spree was it. I hope this isn't the only store she has hit."

"I wouldn't care what kind of man he was. If he could pay my bills like he does Blair's, he could do whatever the hell he wanted to do. If he wanted to have someone on the side, then I would do the same." Lita took her mirror from her jacket pocket to check her makeup. "She let him off too easy. I know nothing takes the place of the comfort of a man, but platinum Visa is a good substitute. She should have held on to this bad boy. Men are all the same. You just don't want to admit it, Denise." Lita picked up an envelope and placed the card inside. She found Justin's number in the Rolodex and picked up the phone to dial the number. "Do you think he'll let me use this card?"

"Here I go again," said Denise. "Why, why, why do I have to be in close contact with women who feel desperate to have just any man or who just wants any man because he has a bank load of money? Where are all of the smart, self-sufficient women?" Denise looked up at the ceiling and shook her head from side to side. "I know you're not going to ask that man that?" Denise moved her head from side to side again to relieve the tension she felt coming on. "Because if you do, you're worse than the other women he has been seen out with."

"He doesn't have to be seen out with me for me to spend his money." Lita closely inspected the Visa card that she had taken back out of the envelope. She ran her fingers across the embossed lettering and numbers.

"What makes you think Justin would want you?" Denise was about to say something else, but a faint popping sound made her stop. "Did you hear that?"

Lita didn't respond to her question. She was busy fantasizing about money, clothes, and cars. "All he's doing is taking advantage of those women. He does it because he can. He uses them and when he's through, he's off to someone else." Lita flipped the card over and over in her hand. "I have never held one of these. I see them a lot, especially from Blair. She comes in and slides it through the machine like it's nothing." Lita cut her eyes at Denise.

"Damn, Lita, Blair just walked out the door and you're ready to ride Justin into the sunset." Denise walked to the racks to re-hang a couple of dresses that had fallen on the floor.

"I don't want to ride him yet, Denise. I have to see if he will let me update my wardrobe first. Let me bring you up to speed, Denise," Lita said in a counseling tone. "Those women are not hanging around Justin just because of his good looks and sexy body. Every woman in town knows Justin is a dog. It's the money, girl. See, what you have to do with a man like Justin is to let him think he is running the show. Justin is so rich that he doesn't realize how much money goes through his hands. He's too busy trying to get busy with as many women as he can, and we women own the business. Trust me, he is not getting off cheap."

"Well don't forget the jewelry." Denise walked towards the window to see what was going on outside and to see where the popping sound came from. There were more people than usual gathered on the corner when she pulled back the curtains on the boutique window.

Lita was eyeing a pair of diamond earrings as she dialed Justin's number. The phone continued to ring. She was hoping Justin would answer. "I'm not going to come out and ask him if I can use his card," she said. "Somehow I will ease it into the conversation when I call him to let him know Blair accidentally left it here. I've seen the way he looks at me when he's in here. And I'm doing nothing wrong. Didn't you hear Blair say that she doesn't want him anymore? Do you think I plan on working here forever?"

"Blair didn't say that she didn't want him," Denise said. "So, I guess you're just working here to find a husband?" Denise continued to peer out of the window.

"Well, Blair implied it," Lita said. "And no, I'm not looking for a husband. Getting married isn't on my agenda. I just need men to help me with my living expenses. Right now I'm in between men." Lita hung up and re-dialed Justin's number.

Denise came away from the window, walked over to the counter, and leaned against it. "So what do you do when a man gets fed up with having to foot the bill? Don't tell me that it doesn't happen, because if I was a man, I don't care how much I loved someone, I don't want to feel like I'm their winning lottery ticket."

Lita was becoming impatient. Justin hadn't answered the phone. "To answer your question, there are plenty of men around who don't mind spending their money when they have more than they need." Lita listened as the phone continued to ring. "And if they ever run out of money or choose not to spend it on me anymore, guess what? There's always a rich unhappy husband or an unhappy man with a girlfriend who thinks that if he finds the right woman who can give him what he's missing at home, he won't mind spending his money on her."

Denise looked at Lita with questioning eyes. "So if a single man with money wanted to marry you, would you?"

"Hell no," Lita said.

"There are some good men out there, Lita. So if a good man asked you to marry him, are you telling me you would turn him down?" Denise asked.

Justin was not answering his cell. His voice mail came on; she didn't leave a message and slammed the phone down. "Denise, do you have a boyfriend?"

"No." There was a hint of attitude in Denise's raised voice.

"Why not?" The tone in Lita's voice was meant to irritate Denise.

"They cheated on me, but that doesn't mean that all men are the same." Denise glanced at Lita and saw the smirk on her face.

"Okay, I will give you that one." Lita tapped her pen on the counter. "How many serious boyfriends have you had in your lifetime?"

"More than a few, and yes they all cheated." Denise crossed her arms. She was becoming defensive. "And I have cut all ties with them. I don't need to be hating on a man to take care of myself."

"What about your daughter?" Lita tucked her hair behind her ears and then folded her hands in front of her waiting for an answer.

Denise had a frown on her face. "What about her?"

"You've never mentioned her father." Lita looked at her with raised eyebrows. "As a matter of fact, you don't talk about her much." Lita playfully tugged on the bracelet that dangled from her wrist. "Does he pay child support?"

Denise unfolded her arms. "What does Nicole's father have to do with this conversation?" She positioned her hands on her waist.

"Everything. He's a man." Lita stared long and hard at Denise. "You're working two jobs to support you and your daughter. That's no way to live, Denise."

Denise inhaled deeply, and then exhaled. "I care not to talk about that part of my life." She saw Lita staring at her. "Why don't you have a man?"

"Well, I have had four relationships that I thought were serious. I was faithful, trusting, always there until I realized that I was just plain naïve." Lita paused to keep her voice from getting any louder. "Every last one of them cheated on me, and for a long time I always thought it was because of something that I did or didn't do." Lita kept staring at Justin's credit card. She held it up to her lips and kissed it. "The only thing I didn't do was take advantage of them."

"You're so crazy, standing up there kissing on a credit card," Denise said. She watched Lita stare at the credit card she held tightly in her hand.

That's okay," Lita said. "Call me what you want, but I'm not stupid like I used to be. You're walking around here telling me that there are some good men in this world." Lita's eyes were seriously scanning the boutique. "You know what? You're right. There are some good men. Let's see," she said while looking up in the air. "There are men who are good at working and keeping a roof over their family's head, good at keeping a job while they have more than one woman and making sure they don't know about each other. Yeah, Denise you're right. You know, some husbands are even good at sleeping with their girlfriend and coming home sleeping with their wife the same night without missing a beat." Lita coughed slightly to clear her throat. Her mouth was dry from her quick rant. "Go ahead and get yourself a real good man. Have you in your lifetime run across a man who has not cheated?"

Denise didn't answer. None of her relationships had been good. If Lita would get off the subject, she could get rid of the headache the conversation caused.

Lita took that as a no. "So if you don't know any faithful men, how in the hell can you tell me there are faithful men out there? Where are they? Show me." Lita looked at Denise and waited for her to give her an answer, any answer. She could see that the truth hurt Denise. She could see it by the look on Denise's face. "You're a big girl, now. Open up your eyes," Lita said.

"You know what, Lita? You blame all men for what some men do. You use them and when you're through, you move on to the next one. You don't even try to love." Denise walked over to the water cooler, pulled a paper cup from the dispenser, and filled it halfway. She stared into the cup before taking a sip. "I once had a friend like you who used men for money. Why not try love?"

"Why should I?" Lita picked up the boutique catalog, flipped through a couple of pages, and laid it back on the counter. "No one loves me. Do you know how many times I have loved a man and tried to get him to love me? As much as I hate to work, I would have dug ditches in the hot sun, if I had a faithful man to come home to. Every boyfriend that I had will tell you that I was the best thing that ever happened to them and that they were the ones that messed up." Lita's voice started to quiver. She hated when her voice sounded that way. She did not want the wall she had built up around her to start tumbling down. "All that I did was for nothing."

"You're just a hater." Denise inhaled and raised her hands above her to relieve some of the tension that built up in her body during the conversation while trying desperately not to agree with Lita.

"You're right." Lita was fidgeting with the emerald earring in her left ear. "I hate all men, but I'm good at not letting them know that and still get what I want."

Suddenly, the door to the boutique flew open so quickly that it startled both of them since they were the only two people in the store.

"My mother. . . my. . . call the ambul. . ." the young boy was stuttering so badly that Lita and Denise could barely understand him. He held on to the end of the counter trying to catch his breath. Denise grabbed the boy by his shoulders in an attempt to calm him. "What's wrong? What do you need?"

"My mother sent me. We need an ambulance. Someone is hurt on the corner. Call 911. Hurry! Please!" He turned and bolted back out the door as fast as he had come in.

Lita already had the 911 operator on the phone and was giving her the location as she looked at the crowd from the side store window. They were gathered around a car. She saw a man pulling someone from the driver seat of the car. After giving the operator all the information, she and Denise locked the store and ran down the sidewalk to see what happened.

After running about a quarter of a block, they saw a lifeless body lying on the sidewalk with blood spewing from the head. They weren't close enough to see the face. No one could tell if the person was dead or alive. There was no movement from the body at all. A tall, Hispanic man asked if anyone knew who the person was. After he got no response, he walked to the car to look for identification. Just as the man opened the passenger door, Denise screamed. She saw the bags from the boutique that she'd handed to Blair before she walked out of the door. With clearly focused eyes, she then recognized the lifeless body. "Oh Blair," she screamed. "Why? It couldn't have been that bad. Why did you have to kill yourself?"

Lita stood frozen while Blair was stretched out on the sidewalk with a bullet hole in her head. A gun was clutched in her right hand.

Lita tried to slow the quick movement of her head. She closed her eyes for a few seconds to keep her balance. She didn't want to faint. Her head felt like it was spinning as she hyperventilated. "I told you men are no good. Look at what he made her do. Oh my God, she shot herself. You could have gotten back at him another way." She could not believe what Blair had done—ended her life because of a man. She now figured that killing herself is what Blair meant when she said she would get back at Justin. As many times as she had seen Blair, she never once thought that she was that fragile. She wished that she could have had a chance to explain men like Justin, or all men for that matter, to Blair. A flood of guilt built up inside of her. "This must have been what she meant when she said she was going to get back at Justin," Lita whispered over and over while catching her breath.

A policeman arrived three minutes later, but an ambulance was nowhere in sight. If Blair wasn't dead, she would be by the time it got there.

"Where are you going?" Denise saw Lita quickly walk away. Denise used both of her hands to wipe the tears from her face. *It's happening again,* she thought. She didn't want to think about why she left D.C. She thought she had gotten away from toxic people who were always involved in bad relationships, revenge, or making other people miserable for the rest of their lives. "Lita, come back. Where are you going?"

"I don't know." Lita was pacing around in small circles, and then started walking back to the boutique.

Denise pushed through the crowd, closer to the body. She took a quick glance as she walked through to catch up with Lita. She held her breath to make sure whatever was in her stomach would stay there. "Wait a minute, Lita." She ran to catch up with her.

"No. I don't want to wait. I just want to get away from here." Lita put her hands to her head. "I can't believe it. I just can't believe it. She had a lot going for herself. Justin's just a man. He's not God." She felt her body heat up. "I will never," she said with force, "let a man have that kind of power over me." She looked over at Denise. "Always remember that we," she said, pointing to Denise, then to herself, "are number one, no matter what any man says. I know you don't like the way I do things when it comes to men." Lita was sobbing hysterically. "I can understand if you don't operate like I do when it comes to them, but Denise, never let them walk over you and get away with it. If leaving them is what you have to do, then that's fine for you. But I cost, and I'm not cheap. To be honest, Denise, I hate men and I'm not in the game for love, but they'll never know it." Lita was breathing so hard that her nostrils were flared. "I've been put through too much. Since you're in it for love, let me give you a word of advice." She paused. "Never let a man make you think you're the lucky one because you're with him. Let him know that he isn't the prize, you are." Lita was walking so fast that she was almost running.

Denise ran and caught Lita by the arm. "Slow down," she whispered. Denise then grabbed Lita by both arms to slow her pace. She wanted to calm her down before she had a stroke. Denise had never seen Lita that upset before. She listened to her go on and on about no good men as they walked. Denise wanted Lita to get a hold of herself before they got back to the boutique. She knew the bags in Blair's car would lead a trail to the boutique and the police would be there soon to question them.

Chapter 5

Carole waved her arm to the waitress to get her attention. She was the owner of Carole's boutique and was getting an update on the events that had gone on the last couple of days while she was out of town at a buyer's convention. She had been grilling Lita and Denise for about forty-five minutes about what happened to Blair. "You mean you two couldn't tell there was something wrong with Blair when she left the shop?" Carole waited for an answer. "Maybe if someone would have taken notice of her condition, she would still be alive today."

"We feel bad enough, Carole. You act like we're criminals or something. I'm not into reading people's mind or the expressions on their faces." Lita stared at Carole for a few seconds and then cut her eyes to Denise. "Can you tell her we would have tried to intervene if we thought Blair was going to shoot herself?"

Denise unfolded her napkin, took the utensils out, and laid them on the table. She put the napkin in her lap. "We didn't notice that she was distraught, Carole." Denise put her elbows on the table and put her face in her hands. "I wish, I really wish we could have known what she was going to do."

"Justin must be going out of his mind," Lita said. "It has to be eating him alive to know that Blair is no longer around." Justin hadn't responded to the messages she left him regarding his charge card. That was the real reason for her concern.

Denise rolled her eyes. She could tell by Lita's tone that she wasn't concerned about how Justin felt. She just wanted what she hoped to get out of him—money. "Were you able to get in touch with Justin?" Denise asked.

Carole sat her cup down and turned to Lita. "Why were you trying to contact Justin?"

"No particular reason," Lita said quickly as she glanced at Denise. *Denise, that discussion about Justin was between me and you,* she thought.

"Sorry, I wasn't trying to spread your business," Denise responded as if she had read Lita's thoughts to keep her mouth shut.

Carole took off her glasses, folded them, and laid them on the table. She slowly picked up the menu and opened it. "Grilled Tilapia sounds good," she said as she perused the menu. "I think I will also have a large Margarita. Anyone else want one? I'm buying." She would get her answers about Lita and Justin one way or another, she thought. She really wasn't interested in what happened to Blair. Justin's funds were her only concern. "Let's order," she said. "And the meal is on me, too."

While waiting for their food, Carole tried to get as much information about what was going on with Justin since Blair's death. "So, how's Justin doing?" She threw the question out not aiming for a particular person. Denise told her that she had not seen Justin since Blair died. Lita didn't respond. She kept drinking and was on Margarita number two.

"Lita?" Carole asked. "What about you? Have you seen Justin lately?" Carole couldn't help but wonder why Lita was trying to get in touch with him. Carole knew Justin was single and had a hard time being without a woman and she knew that Justin was so free with his money because she had dated him a few times.

"No," Lita answered quickly. "I have no reason to see him unless he comes into the boutique." She picked up the folded napkin on the table. She snapped it opened and placed it on her lap to replace the one that had fallen off when she shifted in her seat. "What's with all the questions about Justin? I thought you wanted information on Blair and why we somehow couldn't read her thoughts."

"You two always seem to have something to talk about when he comes into the boutique." Carole was trying to see if there was another connection between Justin and Lita besides Justin being a customer at the boutique when he bought items for Blair. Even though Carole had plenty of money and a successful business, she chose not to spend any of her money on herself. She always used other people's money to take care of her needs and banked hers. Every man that she gives the time of day to has to have his pockets lined with just as much money as she has. Carole knows that she is seriously addicted to other people's money and she had no problem with that. She was going to find out what Lita's plans were for Justin.

"We do have a conversation when he comes into the boutique," Lita said with emphasis. "Other than that, I don't see him or talk to him." Lita wanted to keep her tone the same throughout the questioning. She wanted Carole to stop digging for additional information. It didn't work.

"Wow," Carole said. "I didn't mean to hit a nerve."

"Don't worry, you didn't." Lita sighed loudly. "I talk to most of the customers who come into the boutique. That's part of my job, isn't it?"

Carole didn't answer. She smiled and nodded her head. During her conversation with Lita and Denise over dinner, Carole picked up that Lita too was going after Justin. Even though Lita denied that she was anything more than customer friendly to Justin, Carole didn't buy it. She was going to have to find a way to take Lita out of the equation.

"Can we talk about something else?" Denise clasped her hands behind her head and arched her back to relieve tension she felt building up. She wanted to get the conversation off a man and surely didn't want to get on the subject of relationships.

"Sure," Carole said. "What's going on in your life?" Carole leaned back in her chair and looked at Denise who was taking her time answering the question. She watched as Denise fiddled with her fingers. Carole tapped her own fingers lightly on the table.

Denise bit down softly on her bottom lip, while trying to think of something to say. She didn't want to talk about herself. There was nothing going on in her life. She had the same old routine. Go to work and then go back home. It was the same thing every day. She looked to her right and saw the waiter coming with their food. "Nothing's going on in my life," she said. "Here comes our food, right on time. I'm starved." She managed to divert the conversation from herself while the waiter placed their food on the table. After he finished placing their food in front of them, they all made small talk about other things while attempting to enjoy their meal.

Carole paid for the dinner and everyone went their separate ways. Three was a crowd and Carole wanted to add Justin to her collection of rich men, but Lita was in the way. Trying to get into a man's bed and eventually his bank account was a full time job. She did not want it to become more complicated with other women attempting to do the same thing.

After dinner, Carole got into her red Escalade. Every two years, a new vehicle was at her disposal courtesy of Eric Bastrop. She met him five years ago when she went with a friend who was looking to purchase a new vehicle. After she saw how Eric was checking her out, she then decided she wanted a new vehicle too. She started dating Eric, who was general manager of a Cadillac dealership. Carole liked the way Eric made sure she rode in the best. Before she met him, she was riding around in a nine year old Chevrolet Cavalier, with one hubcap missing. The carpet was spotted with coffee stains. Her car took a full eleven seconds to reach fifty miles per hour. A couple of times she was almost rear-ended when her putt-putt entered the freeway on- ramp. The vehicle still looked good on the outside, but all of the hoses were taped with black electrical tape and there was a slow leak in the radiator. Every two days she had to fill it with water and coolant. The big SUV she was riding in now was a welcome change for her.

Carole was also dating Keith who owned a high-rise in the uptown part of Houston. She met him while they were getting their vehicles detailed one Saturday afternoon. After she noticed how he too was checking her out, she struck up a conversation with him. Once she learned that he owned a high-rise, she decided she wanted to move. Now Carole lived in one of the units, rent-free with a nice view of downtown at night. There was no more looking out of an apartment window into the window of another apartment across the way, where she previously lived with her no good husband. Every night there was some drama going on either in her apartment or someone else's. She and her ex-husband argued constantly. They were verbally abusive to each other on an equal basis. One could not outdo the other when it came to the war of words. She called him a sorry, good for nothing man who wasn't capable of making an above average living. She didn't care if all of the bills were paid and they still had at least five hundred dollars left after all of the necessities were taken care of. She wanted more and told him he was inadequate because he could not provide more. He told her she wasn't even worth what he was already giving her and that's why he didn't and wouldn't attempt to do more. All anyone had to do was open a window and pull up a chair for a ringside view on any particular night. When her husband left her for another woman and left her with everything in the apartment, she left a week later without taking any of the raggedy contents with her. Keith really hooked her up with furniture and the works.

Carole's third boyfriend, Nick, was vice president of Hartwell bank, so she had several credit cards with no limit, and no responsibility for paying them. Carole could buy what she wanted, when she wanted, as long as she was around when Nick wanted her. She came around when she wanted to, but had Nick thinking he was in control. She was just that good. Carole remembered two years ago, how she had been up to her neck in debt. Her husband had run off with a young girl, just out of high school. He had gotten cash advances on all of their credit cards. She met Nick when she had to go into the bank to find out how much of her husband's debt she was responsible for. She poured the charm on Nick and he was hooked like a fish. Just like the rest, she didn't love him either.

She would hold on to Nick the longest because he had the bankroll. Eric kept her riding and Keith kept a roof over her head, but neither of them had the kind of money that would supply her every need. They weren't millionaires.

Carole could see herself never working for anyone again. After she put it on Nick, all of her financial problems were solved. But at this point in her life, Carole was afraid to put all her trust and heart into one man. She had been burned once, twice would put her over the edge. She knew her relationship with Nick wouldn't last very long, for that matter the other men would not be in her life forever either. She was heartbroken, but not dumb. The credit cards given to her by Nick helped her finance the opening of her boutique. The boutique was doing so well that she had a nice little nest egg stashed and a lot more in profits coming in from her business. So those men were not needed on a long-term basis. They were her seeds. She was already looking for someone with more money to replace Nick. He was in the running for now. Justin would be discarded too, as soon as someone with more comes along. She knew you could only hate on a man for so long before he catches on to the game.

Carole started the engine of her candy apple red Escalade, pulled down the visor, and checked her face in the mirror. Since she had just finished lunch, her lipstick needed reapplying. She refreshed her makeup and dabbed more perfume on herself. Carole was not vain, but finally realized that she should not feel guilty about taking care of herself and knowing that she is just as good as anyone else. She realized that she should be able to enjoy the finer things in life and not feel guilty because other people aren't as fortunate as she is.

Carole was her own worst enemy. Most of the time, she was her only enemy. She would often think people were watching what she had on, how she wore her hair, if her shoes matched her outfit, if she would look stupid for running for a class office, homecoming queen, twirler, or cheerleader. What she thought other people would think about her kept her from pursuing things her friends achieved. She always stood silently in the background cheering them on, wishing it were she. Her imagination did a terrible thing to her. It, not the people around her, made her high school and college days two of the most uneventful phases of her life. If she wasn't absolutely sure she could succeed at something, she wouldn't attempt to do it. The fear of failure kept her in the *poor old me* mentality for most of her life.

Tap, tap, tap. The woman tapping on the window of her vehicle startled Carole. She let the window halfway down. "Yes, may I help you?"

"Yes ma'am, I was wondering if you were coming out. I want to park in this space."

Carole looked at the Hispanic woman who spoke broken English. She could tell by her eyes that she was unhappy. Carole watched her as she walked back to her car. The car was familiar. It wasn't a nine-year-old Chevrolet Cavalier, but it was old, probably with coffee stains on the carpet, taped up hoses, and a hole in the radiator. "Yes, I'm coming out," she yelled out of her window. "It is all yours." Carole watched her as she tugged forcefully on her car door to get it open. It took seconds, which seemed like minutes for the woman to get the car to back away to let Carole out of her space. The same putt-putt motion of the car was all too familiar to Carole. *It won't be long before she becomes a hater too,* Carole thought as she backed Big Red out of the space and zoomed off.

Chapter 6

Arlene had succeeded in not letting Justin go to work the past week after their little argument. Justin had come back that Wednesday night. It was now the following Wednesday. She and Justin had their outings during the day, but she kept him under lock and key at her home with her sexual escapades during the nights. She made him feel like a king. She was at his beck and call. She was putting the second part of her plan into motion.

Even after going back to Arlene's, Justin still didn't think he was doing anything wrong. He wasn't even scared of Arlene attacking him again or worried about having enough nerve to face Blair. He hadn't tried to get in touch with her since their last argument, which was seven days ago. He decided to stay away from his place for a while. He figured that Blair was so mad at this point, that she might have a hit out on him.

"What's wrong, Justin?" That was Arlene's favorite question to ask him. "I know what you need?" She sat straddled legged across him while he sat in the dining room chair.

Justin held her by the waist. "What is it that I need?" He heard her answer his question, but he was not paying attention to what she was saying. His mind was on Blair at the moment. A little guilt was starting to set in. Sex hadn't been good with Arlene the last couple of days. Lately, he's been thinking of what his excuse to Blair would be. He was too busy thinking at that point to enjoy himself and had just been going through the motions. He wanted to relax, so he decided to wait until later to figure out what he was going to tell Blair.

Arlene circled her tongue around his ear and down the side of his neck. She took his hand and placed it under her blouse. "Squeeze it," she whispered.

Justin cupped her breast in his hand, barely squeezing. "What is it that I need?" he asked again.

"You need me, only me," Arlene whispered as she blew in his ear. All Justin was to her was money in the making. Arlene didn't give a damn about anyone. "Come on, let's ride down to Galveston. Even though it's the end of November, it has warmed up since last week." Arlene stood up, raised her skirt to reveal the bikini she had on under it.

Justin looked at her with a slight grin on his face. "Well, I guess I'd better go get dressed." He was still afraid to go to his place. Justin excused himself and went into the bathroom. He thought about how it didn't take much to make Blair happy, yet he stilled lavished her with gifts and money, but so little of him. Her words were always encouraging. She never put him down. She was always putting him on a pedestal. He could not understand why he couldn't do right by her. Blair meant everything to him. He wished the curse that he believed he inherited from his father would just disappear. When he actually thought about how he treated women, he didn't like it. Othertimes, he was consumed with himself that he didn't notice it. At this moment, he wondered what the hell he was doing there with Arlene.

Justin locked the bathroom door and turned on the shower. He took out his cell phone and dialed Blair's number. He actually missed her so much that he could hardly think straight. He was quickly trying to think of what he was going to say to her while the phone was ringing. This time he did not have a pre-rehearsed answer. Blair's answering machine came on. He was about to leave a message when the phone was picked up. He wasn't prepared for what was said on the other end.

"You no good son-of-a-bitch," the voice said. "What took you so long to call? I have been leaving messages at your home for a week and you haven't bothered to call back." She stopped to catch her breath in between sobs. "You haven't been to work for a long while. I know because I have been to your job and to the gym. Your ass sure knows how to disappear when you don't want to be found. You even have your employees lying about not knowing your whereabouts."

The rambling went on and on. Justin started to hang up the phone, but he decided to wait it out and get it over with. He no longer had on his mind how much he missed Blair. The ranting on the phone changed his mood. He tightened his jaw and gripped the phone. He released the tension in his hand to make sure the phone didn't come apart. "Who the hell do you think you're talking to?" he yelled. Justin wanted to put his fist through Arlene's bathroom wall. "I don't owe you any explanation about what I do, where I go, or who I'm with." He huffed. He sat on the edge of the tub and leaned forward as he took a deep breath. "Listen, this is the last—" He was interrupted.

"I'm talking to you!" There was a break in the signal. "Hello, damn it. Are you still there?" Janice's breathing became heavy. "Yeah, I'm talking to you in case you didn't hear me the first time." Her heels made clicking noises against the kitchen floor. She couldn't stand still. She rubbed her forehead with her index finger and thumb. "I can't believe you took this long to call back. You're a poor excuse for a man." Janice couldn't slow her breathing. It was hard for her to pace the floor and talk at the same time.

Justin couldn't take the insults any longer. "Janice, will you shut the hell up and put you sister on the phone? Our business is not your business." *I can't believe Blair called her sister again. I wish she would keep other people out of our business.*

"You son-of-a-bitch, it is my business. What you have done to my sister has made it my business. I could kill you, Justin. Do you hear me? If I ever see you again, you're a dead man. You'd better stay the hell away from me." She was screaming hysterically. "It's all your fault. You're a heartless man."

Justin rolled his eyes and then closed them tightly. He had been through this before with Janice, even though they only met twice. "Okay, Janice, what the hell do you want me to do? Yeah, I messed up, again, but this is between Blair and me. Since you want to stick your nose into our business, tell me what you want me to do." He chuckled.

There was silence on the phone. She tried to calm herself before speaking again. It was so painful for her to talk to Justin. The suffocating feeling she got from talking to him made her want to faint. She closed her eyes tightly and regained her composure. She heard Justin chuckle. "Oh, so this is funny to you, huh Justin?" She tried to slow her breathing. Janice's voice was cracking as she began to speak. After a couple of seconds, she was able to speak again. "You know what, Justin?" Janice paused. "Do what you would do when the one you say you love is dead."

There was silence. Janice didn't know if Justin was in shock or if he was trying to come up with a good lie. She hung up the phone before Justin could say anything. It didn't matter what he said. It wouldn't bring Blair back. She figured Justin wasn't sorry for the way he had treated Blair. He is just *sorry* period. Janice put her hand on her chest under her left breast bone. She pressed her thumb into the area and moved it in a circular motion. She wanted the pain to go away. She couldn't tell if it was a physical pain she was feeling or heartache from losing Blair. Her only sister was gone. She was all alone with no family. Their mother and father had died six and ten years ago. After their deaths, she packed up and moved to Phoenix, while Blair stayed in Houston. Even though they were far away in distance, they were very close in their relationship. Three years ago she came back to Houston and moved not far away from Blair. They only had each other until Justin came into the picture. Then Janice had no one. She disliked him the moment she met him. She noticed that he had a certain arrogance about himself that made him think that he was the best looking man to walk the earth. She couldn't stand to be around him. Janice avoided Justin whenever possible. She and Blair had many discussions concerning Justin, but after a while, Janice realized that Blair had to learn the hard way. She never imagined that the lesson would kill her only sister.

Janice had her own issues to deal with. Blair had always been there for her. She was her rock of Gibraltar. Janice couldn't imagine herself going on her long walks alone. Blair helped her to keep her head clear and tried to help her get through her stressful days. Janice's head started to hurt. Her heart started to beat faster. Withdrawal symptoms were overtaking her. Her intense craving for liquor and sweets had resurfaced. She went from cabinet to cabinet in Blair's apartment. Nothing. Her drugs of choice were nowhere to be found. "Blair," she screamed. "Help me!" Janice looked around at the pictures on the wall. That was the only way she would be able to see Blair again. Her tears flowed heavily. She knew she could no longer count on Blair. Blair had not been with her long enough to help her deal with her addictions. It was so difficult for Janice not to give in. She went to the refrigerator and grabbed a bottle of water and gulped it down. There was no one she could call. Her sister was her only support system. They were trying to handle it on their own. Her craving became stronger and stronger until she just couldn't take it anymore. She suddenly found herself with keys in hand. The Dessert Factory was only a seven-minute drive away and the liquor store was two doors away from it. She walked her 238-pound frame to her SUV and drove off.

Chapter 7

The miserable winter had come and gone. It didn't look like spring was going to be much better. None of Justin's clothes fit him anymore. Buying more clothes was the last thing on his mind. He had barely left his house in three and a half months. He was fortunate enough to have competent people running his construction business, since he had not been to work more than three days a week since Blair's death. He did not have the initiative to do anything. Food, sex, work, or anything physical wasn't a priority with him.

He had gotten so many calls from women that he didn't bother to answer his phone anymore. He let the answering machine pick up his messages. His best friend, Leonard, had been trying to get in touch with him for weeks. Justin would text him back to let him know that he was doing fine. He didn't want anyone coming to his house to check on him. His weight loss made him look like he had been on crack for years. He was twenty pounds lighter and the weight loss took away from his physique. He had lost some of his muscle tone and his belly started to get a little bulge. His six pack stomach was gone. He barely ate, but spent most of his time trying to drink away his pain. His stock was almost gone. He drank and slept for days on end.

He didn't look forward to getting up in the morning. He told his housekeeper months ago to take a vacation and he would let her know when it was over. He still made sure she received her weekly pay-check. His house wasn't dirty; it was filthy. He barely ate, but when he did eat, he would throw the containers or pizza boxes on the floor wherever he happened to be sitting or lying at the time. He would bathe, sit in the tub for hours until he was wrinkled, thinking how he would never get another chance to do right by Blair. The last time he had seen her was during their last argument. It hurt him that their last time together had not been spent in love and peace. He had stayed out of touch for so long after their last encounter, that he missed her funer-al. He could imagine what people were saying. He was her man and was nowhere to be found. He was with Arlene the whole time and she made sure everyone in town knew it. He couldn't bring himself to face anyone. Lots of people speculated that Blair took her life to make his miserable, to get his attention as she said many times. The talk of the town was that he drove her to killing herself. It hurt his heart deeply that he didn't even get the chance to say goodbye. He thought about their last time together as he dressed to go to the bank. He hoped he would be through crying before he walked out the door.

Justin wanted to get in and out of the bank before anyone saw him.

He slowly shuffled to the counter where the deposit and withdrawal slips were located. His head was positioned downward so that he wouldn't have to make eye contact with any of the bank customers or employees. All eyes were on him as he picked up the chained, ball-point pen from the counter. He struggled to separate the withdrawal slips until he was able to pick up only one. He looked sideways to the right and caught a glimpse of two women who were in line staring at him. He quickly glanced back down at the withdrawal slip he had in his hand, wrote in an amount, and slowly walked to the end of the line with his head still bowed. Five minutes had passed until he made it to the teller and handed her the withdrawal slip. He stood in front of her, but not looking directly at her as she counted out his money.

"One hundred, two hundred, three hundred, four hundred, five hundred, six hundred, seven hundred, eight hundred dollars." The teller put the money in the envelope and handed it to Justin. "Is there anything else I can do for you?" the teller asked. Since he didn't answer, she took that as a no. "Goodbye, Mr. Vanderbilt, and you have a good day."

The money looked so familiar to Justin because he had plenty of it. It never stayed in his hands long because he was always giving it to Blair. Eight hundred dollars was about how much he gave her each week to spend on herself, but to him she was worth it. He knew she didn't spend that much money in a week. She wasn't interested in being high maintenance. She was banking it and he knew it. To him, giving Blair money had justified all the wrong he did to her. It was his guilt-reliever. He took four of the one hundred-dollar bills and stuck them in his wallet. "Just a moment, Miss. I want to put this back in." Justin turned back around and laid the rest of the money on the counter and picked up a deposit slip that was in front of the teller's window and filled it out. He was so used to getting enough money for Blair, that he had not realized he was now only making a withdrawal for one.

As Justin walked out of the bank, he remembered a message that Lita had left on his machine months ago. "*Hello Justin, this is Lita. I am so sorry about what happened to Blair. My heart goes out to you. If there is anything that I can do to help you, please don't hesitate to call. I know you miss her very much. She was such a beautiful woman. I hope you continue to shop at the boutique, well scratch that, we have no men clothing but we would love to see you again. By the way, Blair must have dropped your Visa by accident. I have it here at the boutique for you to pick up when you are in the area. I would have mailed it, but didn't want to take a chance of it being lost in the mail. If you would like for me to drop it off to you, I would be happy to do that. Hope to hear from you soon.* As painful as it would be for him to go there, he knew he should go pick up his card.

The drive to Carole's boutique took less than half an hour. Justin was used to having Blair in the car with him whenever he was on this side of town. He was like most men when it came to shopping. He didn't like to go shopping with Blair, only because she wasn't in and out of a store quick enough for him. She seemed so happy trying on outfits and modeling them for him and he pretended to love watching her. Now he wished he could have those times back. He missed her so much. If he could have just another chance, he tried to convince himself that he would be a different man. But the little voice in the back of his head kept telling him that his good boy routine would not last long. It wasn't in him. He could hear female voices as he got out of his car. He watched the women come out of the boutique and other stores next to it. Justin leaned against his car watching the women. They seemed to be walking in slow motion. His mind kept telling him if he stood there long enough, Blair would come walking out with an armload of bags. He kept waiting and looking, waiting and looking. He waited and looked for fifteen minutes. Blair just wouldn't come out of one of the many stores lining the street.

"Justin." He felt a hand on his arm, which made him almost jump to the other end of his car. It was Denise standing there with a bag of food from the Chinese restaurant from across the street. "How are you? It's been so long." Denise caught him by the hand, prompting him to walk with her. "Are you all right?" She was almost pulling him, forcing him to take steps. "I didn't mean to scare you. Let's go inside."

He was stilled dazed. He was standing still, but he felt as if he was moving in slow motion and going nowhere. He didn't know if he answered her or not. He could hear Denise's voice, but saw Blair's face. Denise was still talking; he wasn't interested in her conversation. He didn't know why he had gone to the bank or even left the house for that matter. He felt useless. He came out of his trance. "Did I lock my car door?" Justin turned around and hit the lock button on his key chain, then the unlock button, then the lock button again. He started walking back toward his car. "I'll be right back." He got to the door, pulled the handle. It didn't open. He looked up at the street sign as if he had parked in an unfamiliar place and needed to know where to find his car. He looked at the street signs that said Varner and Hastings Street. He wondered why those names keep rolling around in his head. He had seen this intersection thousands of time, but for some reason, it kept haunting him.

Denise sat her food on top of the mailbox and walked back over to Justin who was wrestling with guilt. He was bent over with his hands on the hood of his car shaking his head back and forth. He realized he was standing at the very corner where Blair killed herself. "Come on, Justin." Denise took his hand and he walked slowly with her towards the boutique. She turned to get her food, but saw a homeless man standing at the mailbox eagerly tearing into the bag. She felt sorry for him and kept walking.

Once inside the boutique, Justin walked to his favorite area where he used to sit while Blair did her shopping. Denise walked away as soon as Justin sat down and put his face in his hands. He couldn't control himself any longer. "I miss her. I really, really miss her. I would do anything to have her standing right here, right now." After a couple of minutes of talking to himself, Justin took control of his emotions. He surely didn't want to start crying. He was afraid to display any emotion and he didn't care what people thought of him if he didn't. To him, emotion was a sign of weakness.

All eyes were on him and at this point, he didn't care. Lita approached Justin with a box of tissue and a glass of water. Even though she should have been working, she ignored the customers who were in the store and kept her focus on Justin. When she reached the chair he was sitting in, she knelt beside it and handed him a tissue to wipe his face. "Would you like something to drink?" She tried to give the drink to him, but he would not look up. She got up from her kneeling position, sat in the chair beside him, and put her arm on his shoulder. "Justin, you need to take care of yourself or have someone do it for you. Look at your clothes, they're all wrinkled, and it looks like you haven't eaten for months." Lita used her hands to pull Justin's head on her chest as she turned to face him. "Let me know when you're ready for company, and I'll come and help you out. I really don't mind. Okay, Justin? I mean it. Don't hesitate to call me for any reason."

Denise kept her eyes on Lita. She watched as Lita put her plans in motion for Justin. That was all she talked about since Blair's death. She noticed that Lita even went out and got a new hairstyle, clothes, and jewelry—the works. Lita went and *hated* on some poor vulnerable man who had just enough money to get her what she wanted until she snagged Justin. She knew Lita would hold on to Justin long enough to get enough money out of him until she could wing it on her own for a while. She wasn't looking for a long-term commitment, just long money.

"Here, take this, Justin." Lita gave the glass of water to Justin as he raised his head from her chest.

Denise continued to watch Lita as she tried her best to get him to open up to her or at least convince him that he needed some female attention. Denise now felt that it was her fault for leading Justin into a trap. "I should have left him outside," she said to herself.

"I don't need anything. I'm okay, but thank you." He sat the glass on the table next to him. "This place reminds me too much of her." Justin stood up and walked toward the counter. "I just came to get my credit card that Bla . . ," He could barely say her name.

Lita followed him. She went behind the counter, opened the drawer, and took out the envelope that contained the card. She walked over to Justin and took one of his hands. "Here, Justin." She pressed it firmly in his hand, then took his arms and put them around her waist.

Denise watched her as she whispered something in his ear. She saw Justin nod his head, put the card in his wallet, and head for the door.

"Bye, Justin, take care," Lita yelled in an uncaring tone. Smiling, she watched Justin as he continued out the front door of the boutique. She leaned on the counter with her right hand on her hip, thinking about how long it will take Justin to get over Blair. He was taking much longer than she had wanted to wait.

Denise's eyes darted back and forth from Lita then back to Justin as he disappeared out the door. She went back to doing her work with a sly grin on her face, seeing that Lita failed at getting Justin to let her use the Visa card.

*****

Even through closed doors, while staring through the glass window, the clanking of the metal plates was easy to hear. The gym was filled with men and women pumping iron, running on the treadmills, and riding on the stationary bikes. People were looking at Justin as he looked in. When he left the boutique, he unconsciously walked three blocks past his car to the gym where he used to work out. They all knew who he was, even though he had not been there in three months. His workout schedule used to be like clockwork. He worked out every day from 1:00 p.m. until 3:00 p.m. A couple of the regulars waved to him as he looked in. Justin acknowledged them with a slight nod of his head. *One step at a time,* he kept telling himself. Justin knew he had to come back to life and get back to his normal routine. The love of his life was gone and there was nothing he could do about it. He knew he would never find anyone like Blair, but he did believe that he could love again. He thought about selling his business and going where no one knew him. He knew most of the women he dated were all about money. Every woman, single, married, divorced, widowed, was all after him at this point.

Justin was about to turn around and head back to his car, when something in the window caught his attention. He could see a reflection of a red Escalade sitting at the red light behind him. He knew it was Carole. Even though she wasn't the only person in the city with a red Escalade, everyone knew her vehicle when they saw it. It was always shinier than any vehicle he had seen, especially for a woman. He was hoping she didn't see him, because he did not feel like being bothered. He had gone out with her a couple of times. She was nice and pretty, but not his type. She had money, but to her, the more the better. She hadn't worked too hard to get the money she needed to start her business, at least not 9 to 5. He knew the first time they dated that there was not going to be a relationship. All she talked about was money, investors, and opening a string of boutiques in the city. She was just one of the many women he dated.

He thought about turning around and going back to his car, pretending that he had not seen her or wait for her to pass by. But it was too late; he could hear her blowing her horn. Actually it sounded like she was leaning on it, because it was a continuous sound. "Damn." He turned around to wave to Carole. She waved back to him and went through the green light to pull up to the curb to park. But it wasn't Carole who was blowing the horn. *Where in the heck did she come from?* Arlene was right behind her in her black Infiniti J30. Justin felt water come down the inside of his thighs. He had stood out in the heat so long, he was sweating between the legs. He thought he had peed on himself. It didn't matter if he had or not. He was not committed to either woman, but he knew there was always trouble when the women he dated all meet up together. He knew some drama was about to unfold. He went into his actor mode. *Get it together. Let's see, what can I say? Think man, think. Run, yeah that's it, just take off running.* He seriously considered just hauling ass down the sidewalk, or he could just play the crazy, depressed man that just lost his girlfriend. Now he had it together. When all the questions start about who is she and how long have you known her, he will just stand there and pretend to cry.

This time he didn't care about showing any emotion. He just wanted these vultures to get away from him. His plan was to make them feel sorry for him about Blair's death so that they would back off, at least for today. *Anyway, who are they to question me? They were never my girlfriends. But women don't care. Once they date you, they think they own you.*

Arlene got out of her vehicle first. Carole was still sitting in hers looking into the mirror on her visor. She was putting on lipstick, but Justin knew she was actually watching him. And he was trying to watch Arlene while she was crossing the street and keep an eye on Carole as she sat in her vehicle. He was trying to read the look on Arlene's face, but she was still too far away. But the closer she got, the more her expression changed.

"Well hello, Justin." Arlene stood next to him so that they both were facing the street.

Does she know about Carole, or is she just looking at something across the street? Justin put his left hand in his pocket in case Arlene got the urge to hold it. "I'm doing great. How are you?" Justin wished he had stayed at home.

"I'm doing just fine. I didn't know if you still existed. It has been a while since I last saw or heard from you. And you weren't good company at all. You still look a little shabby. When are you going to go back to your old self?" She was now facing Justin. "What's so interesting across the street?" she asked.

"Nothing." Justin noticed that Carole had not moved. He wondered what she was waiting for. To him the scariest thing about a woman is when she knows something is up, but is slow to react. He could deal with a woman flying off the handle, but when a mad, smiling woman approaches him, he knows he has to think quickly to diffuse the situation. He didn't know if the smile meant that she didn't know anything or if she was going to haul off and knock him in the head when he least expected it. *Maybe I should faint right here, right now on the sidewalk.* He quickly darted his eyes back to Arlene. "What are you doing here?" The slamming of Carole's truck door caught his attention.

Arlene stood directly in front of him to get his full attention. "I came to join the gym. I had to find something to do with my free time and excess energy." She turned back around and looked back across the street. The two women stared each other down as Carole got closer.

Justin watched Carole as she waited for the cars to go by so she could cross the street. *Okay, they see each other. I'll just start crying. Think about Blair.* No matter how hard he tried, he could not make the tears flow. He tried to make himself faint, but he was either too scared or not scared enough. He didn't know which. He told himself he was too much of a man to cry anyway. Lately, he noticed that he had to convince himself of that. His tough exterior was now starting to disintegrate. Almost all of his life he was ruthless without thinking about it. He didn't care about anyone's feelings and felt he owed no one, not even his parents, an explanation about what he did or who he did it with. But now, he wasn't so sure on how much longer he could remain tough.

Carole was now two feet away from them. "Hello, Mr. Vanderbilt. Good to see you again." She gave a quick wave, never acknowledged Arlene, and walked into the gym, where she first met Justin after she gave him her business card to her boutique a year ago.

What? That's it? he thought. "I'm doing fine and it's good seeing you again too," he said. Justin ran his hand unconsciously across his forehead. He didn't know if he was glad or disappointed that Carole didn't make a scene. He started to wonder if he was losing his touch with women.

Arlene bent down to pick up her gym bag off the sidewalk. "I'll be seeing you. I'd better get in and sign up before it gets crowded. I need to pump up my muscles a little bit. I never know when I might need them." She walked in the gym.

Okay, Carole saw me talking to Arlene and she didn't make a scene, but does Arlene know about Carole? She didn't ask any questions when Carole spoke. He stared through the glass window. Everyone was still working out, but more people had come since he last looked in. He saw Carole and Arlene standing in line to check in. No scene, no argument, but both were smiling. Now he was really scared.

Chapter 8

Carole was in the locker room with her mind spinning a hundred miles a minute. She knew there were other women after Justin. This was the second time she had come into contact with the real thing. Carole still wasn't sure if Lita was definitely trying to hook Justin. She really couldn't tell from the little bit of information she got during their lunch a couple of months ago. But she was wondering how far into the hating game the woman outside was with Justin. She had to give it to the girl, she was stunning, but Carole wasn't jealous. Carole knew she was drop dead gorgeous too. She didn't care if that chick got her hooks into Justin, because she didn't care about him or any man. She just wanted to get to him first, get all she could out of him, and then get out. She could have what was left.

The competition walked into the locker room. She looked around and then headed towards a locker three spaces down from Carole's locker. She suddenly had goose bumps and didn't know why. She wasn't intimidated or afraid of Carole. "Is this your first time here?" she asked. "My name is Arlene."

Carole turned away from her locker, looked at Arlene, and turned back around without answering. Even though she didn't know Arlene, she disliked her because they were both after the same man. *I know she isn't talking to me.* She saw no one else in the locker room. *Well, I guess she is.* Carole turned back to look at Arlene again, and again she turned to her locker without answering. *How dare she have the nerve to say anything to me.*

Arlene was puzzled about the two quick glances she got from Carole. She slammed her locker shut. She then carefully laid her comb, brush, and hair tie on the towel she placed on the bench. She carefully brushed her hair back and put it into a ponytail. She looked side eyed at Carole and she saw that she was doing her own thing, and taking her time doing it.

Arlene opened her locker again to place her clothes and hair accessories in her gym bag. She slammed the locker shut again, but harder this time.

Carole jumped at the sound of the locker shutting.

"I guess you heard that," Arlene hissed. "I was just speaking and you're having an attitude. It's women like you that make us look bad." Arlene kicked someone's old tennis shoe that was on the bench on to the floor so she could sit down.

Carole stood up and quietly closed her locker. "Look, Arlene, I didn't come here to make friends, only to work out." Carole draped her white workout towel behind her neck and grabbed the ends of it with her hands. "And furthermore, I'm a loner, don't need any friends, and I don't want any."

Arlene bent over to tie her tennis shoes. "Well sweetie, with all the men you are doing, you don't have time for any friends." Arlene sat up on the bench. "After a while, all of those men you're going through will begin to take a toll on that body of yours," she taunted. "Once you hit that one hundred mile mark, you won't find a man who will be willing to take a test drive. Neither one of us is getting any younger." Arlene caught her reflection in the mirror, suggesting that Carole didn't look as good as she did. Arlene knew all about Carole and her men she hated on. "You have to get a man to trust you enough and you have to play the game well enough to be wife material." Arlene had an art in destroying a woman's self-esteem with her words. But today wasn't the day she chose to break Carole down. She was giving her the mild version.

Carole let go of the towel and turned to face Arlene. "You don't know anything about me." She turned to look at three other women who had just walked into the locker room. She noticed they slowed their pace to see what was going on. Carole made it easier for them to know what was going on. She didn't attempt to lower her voice. "I would advise you to keep your thoughts and opinions about me to yourself."

"You can advise me all you want, but I'm free to say whatever I choose. You just don't have to answer."

"Look," Carole said. "I just came here to work out."

"I think you were following Justin, if you ask me."

"Well I didn't ask you anything."

Arlene adjusted her waistband on her exercise pants. "Face it. We're both after the same thing."

"If you are trying to be a gold digger, honey, you need the right shovels. You don't have to dig so deep if you're only trying to hate on him." Carole was fishing for information without asking Arlene any direct questions.

"I don't need any schooling from you…" she caught herself before the B word left her lips. "I do understand about the hating game. To each his own, but I am playing for keeps. So I will be doing the chasing, not the hating," Arlene said. "If you chase the right way, one man is all you need to get what you want out of life. Being a rich man's wife is your insurance policy for life."

Carole turned around to face Arlene. She let out a slight laugh. "Wife? You are really crazy." She continued to laugh. "You really don't know what you're doing."

"Just because you don't know what I'm doing, doesn't mean I'm not doing it right." Arlene was standing in her favorite show off position. She was standing in the doorway of the locker room with her hands on each side of the doorframe, proud to show off her body. "You don't know what kind of relationship Justin and I have."

Carole was still laughing, only louder this time. "Do you think Justin wants a wife? And if he did, it certainly won't be you. Blair was ten times better than you and he didn't marry her. You're just like me, playing the hating game."

Arlene took about three deep breaths. "I'm nothing like you. You and I have nothing in common."

"I'm sorry, you're right. You're nothing like me." Carole closed her locker door and started walking out of the locker room. Once she got past Arlene, she turned around and said, "You're playing a game that I guarantee you won't win."

"Not so fast. Can I get a word in, or am I too much competition?"

Carole couldn't let that go. She came back in. "Say what you have to say, so I can go do what I came here to do."

"Justin is a narcissistic dog. He doesn't care about anyone's feelings but his. He thinks he's catering to women when he flashes his money around. But in his mind and in his world, everything is all about him."

"Oh really." Carole leaned against a locker.

"Yes, really," Arlene said. "He knows that he can get women with his looks or his money or a combination of both."

"What's wrong with a woman wanting a man with money and looks?" Carole asked.

Arlene sighed. "Everything, if the woman is looking for love. Justin doesn't love anyone," she said with emphasis. "He is in a win-win situation. All he wants is for women to be at his beck and call. The problem is the women that attach themselves to Justin think that he loves them."

Carole continued to listen to Arlene while wishing she would hurry up and get to the end of her sermon.

Arlene kept talking only now at a slower pace. “There are two types of women that fall for Justin. The ones that want to fall in love, be his wife, cook his dinner, wash his clothes, and have his babies. They are the ones that tell themselves that even without the money, they could still love Justin,” she said sarcastically. “He’s so fine, they say, and he looks so good and is everything that I’ve always wanted in a man.”

“And how do you know all of this?” Carole interrupted.

“Because I was one of those women who believed in fairytales. Those women are so blinded by Justin’s insincere devotion to them, his smooth way of talking himself out of any situation that they forgive him.” She paused. “Now us,” she said, pointing to herself then to Carole, “we are the female version of Justin.”

Carole drew in a deep breath, and then exhaled. “We’re nothing alike, Arlene.”

“Yes we are,” Arlene quickly said. “We’re in love with ourselves, we smooth talk our way to get want we want, we flaunt our looks, our bodies, and know that any man in his right mind will not pass up a chance with us. But there are too many of ‘us’ and not enough of the ‘Justin’s’ for us to get our hands on. I know what kind of woman I am, what I want, and how to get it.”

Carole looked up at the clock on the wall and noticed three minutes had passed. “I need to get going. Time waits for no one and I have none to waste on this ridiculous conversation.”

“Okay, run along,” Arlene said. “But remember, we are one of two types of women, the women who hope to have the life they dream to have or the ones who plan to have the life they want. And you say we are not alike, we are exactly alike, and one in the same. But we're big girls, we can go at it hard, but safe. May the one with the best business plan win. Because neither one of us is in it for love nor is Justin."

"Are you done?" Carole asked.

"Almost," Arlene whispered. "I don't need friend's either. When I did have friends, I gave them fair warning—"

"Warning about what?" Carole interrupted.

"I specifically told them if they had a man and if he's rich and they wanted to keep him, not to bring him around me. Now I'm sure you can figure out why I don't have any friends."

Carole put her iPod earplugs in her ear and shook her head while smiling. When Arlene left the locker room after giving her brief business plan talk on how to get a man, Carole leaned against the wall. "Damn," she said to herself. "Arlene's a chaser. If she is successful at hooking Justin, then all of his money will be on lock down." She knew she had to work fast.

Chapter 9

"Mom, pick up the phone." Nicole ran through the living room and jumped onto the sofa with a loud thud. She held the cordless receiver in the air until Denise took it from her hands.

"Why do you do that? Don't plop down so hard on the sofa. Do it again and you'll be sitting on the floor." Denise walked to the other end of the sofa and sat on the arm.

"Sorry," Nicole said.

"Hello."

"Hey girl, what's up?" Gina, her best friend for better or worse, was on the other end.

"I'm washing clothes, vacuuming, and cleaning out the refrigerator. The same thing I do every Friday night." Denise saw Nicole listening while she was pretending to watch television. Nicole's eyes stayed focus on one spot of the television screen. Her tense facial expression and lack of movement gave her away. "Hold on for a second," she said to Gina. "Hey sweetie, go in your room. I need a little privacy."

Nicole picked up the remote and turned off the television. "Yes, ma'am." She picked up her biology book and strolled slowly to her bedroom.

Denise put the phone back to her ear. "Okay, I'm back girl. I had to send Nicole to her room." She let out a sigh. "Sometimes I feel so bad because I can't give her what she wants and half the time I can't even give her the things she needs." Denise glanced down the hallway to make sure Nicole had made it to her bedroom. "She's such a good child. She deserves more."

"What are you talking about? She has a roof over her head, clothes, food, and insurance. I say that you are giving her everything that she needs. Everything else should be secondary. You're always worrying about unimportant things." As soon as those words left Gina's lips, she wanted to take them back. She realized she was on the outside looking in. She had no children that she was responsible for and only had to worry about taking care of herself. How should she know what Nicole needed or how Denise felt about not being able to give her the things a mother wants to give a child. "But I have some extra money if you need it. Come by after four tomorrow evening." She was hoping that would take the edge off the speech she just gave Denise. Gina thought that being generous to her best friend made her feel like she was contributing to the well-being of her goddaughter. Even though she spent very little time with Nicole, she thought she was a great godmother.

"Thanks, Gina. I really appreciate the offer." Denise got quiet for a couple of seconds. "Maybe one of these days I'll be successful like you. If it was just me, I wouldn't worry so much." There was another pause. "I'll come around five. That will give you more time to finish up what you're doing, or should I say who you're doing. Anyway, I know you called for something. It's rare that I hear from you on a Friday night. So, what's going on?"

Gina let out a long sigh. "I've been on the go a lot. You know, Denise, I just thought it was about time for me to slow down and be still for a while. All of this partying every weekend is taking a toll on my mental health and my body. I want to know what it is like to just be still." She let out another long sigh. "I want to hang out with my friends sometimes, like I used to. And no, I won't be doing anybody tomorrow. I have decided to spend the day with my 80-year-old aunt. I miss talking with her. Life is so precious and sometimes so short. She is the only family I have left."

"Is your aunt sick?" Denise asked. "It's been a while since I've seen her. I remember how she used to take us to brunch every other Saturday during our freshman year in college."

"No, but she's just getting up in age. You know when I say life is so short, I didn't mean because Aunt Ellen is old. My life may be short. I don't know how long I'll be around." Gina paused. She was going to say something else, but changed her mind. "I just want to be focused and crystal clear on how I want my life to be and to roll with the punches without all the drama."

Denise took the phone off her ear and looked at it. "Are you coming off your high horse, Gina? What kind of problems could you possibly have? Money problems? No, because you have a thriving temporary service business that is growing every year. Men problems? No. Health problems?" Denise paused. "You're not sick, are you?"

Gina hesitated. "Everyone has problems, Denise, even people with money, and no I'm not sick. I just think about Blair sometimes." Gina sighed heavily. "Even though I didn't know her that well, she stays on my mind. Justin couldn't have been worth killing yourself over. Why would a woman kill herself over a man?" Gina asked. "I just don't understand it. People have the option of living their lives any way they choose and as soon as things don't go their way, they want to go shoot themselves, take an overdose of pills, or sit in the garage in a car with the engine running. And there is no way in hell that I would kill myself over a man." There was a long pause on the phone. Neither of them knew what to say. "Denise, be sure to come and see me tomorrow. I'll have the money here for you. Bring Nicole with you. I would love to see her again."

"Okay, girl. And quit tripping. You're just going through a phase. In a couple of weeks you will be your old self again. Whomever you broke up with this time is not worth you being down about. I don't know who it is, but whenever you want to talk about it, let me know." Denise waited for a response. "Okay?"

Gina blew out a deep breath. "Yeah, maybe we will talk when I see you tomorrow."

"Okay. Love you," Denise said.

Gina hung up the phone and wiped the tears from her eyes. Tomorrow, she would go spend a couple of hours with her aunt. She had an appointment with her lawyer at 1:00 p.m. At 33-years-old, she was about to do something that she hadn't planned on doing until years down the road. Tomorrow afternoon, she would draw up her will. She was dying of cervical cancer.

Denise found herself counting to ten. She truly loved Gina, but Gina could come off as a cruel, mean, bitter person when she didn't choose her words carefully. Denise already knew why Gina acted the way she did. Gina always wanted to be the center of attention. She spared no expenses when it came to herself. She religiously kept her weekly hair, nail, and massage appointments. The more money she made, the more she spent on herself. Occasionally, she would splurge and treat her friends to dinner or a night on the town. She was very good at weeding out the leaches from her true friends. Gina was raised by her Aunt Ellen, since she was an afterthought where her mother was concerned. Her mother thought of her after everything else. Sometimes she would wonder if her mother actually knew she had a child, Gina would often tell Denise. She honestly knew what a motherless child felt like.

Denise went to her refrigerator, then to her pantry. She was taking inventory of her food supply to see what she absolutely needed to get from the grocery store. She kept thinking about Gina. She had never heard her talk like that before. No man has ever made her act the way she was acting. "She'll get over it. A man should be the least of her worries. I'm standing here trying to figure out how to best spend fifty dollars I have budgeted for groceries and she is letting a man make her go off the edge. True, she is not doing what Blair did, but emotional death isn't any better."

An hour later, Denise was looking in the refrigerator and pantry again as if she thought more food had magically appeared. She stood there and called out all the items in the pantry one by one.

Nicole was standing in the doorway listening to her mother. "Who are you talking to?"

"Myself." Denise closed the pantry door. "And why are you standing or should I say hiding by the doorway listening?"

Nicole saw the worried look on her mother's face. Even though she was only17-years-old, she wished that somehow she could make it all go away. She hated seeing her mother go over her bills five or six times or hear the clank of coins her mother would count out nightly just to make sure Nicole had lunch money for the next day. All her mom did was work, come home, worry, go to sleep, and get up the next morning just to do it all over again. "I just came out of my room to get a drink."

Denise walked over and playfully swatted her on the behind. "Okay babe, make sure your room is clean before you go to bed. Tomorrow evening we're going to go see Gina."

That was definitely something that Nicole did not want to do. She did not like Gina and she had a feeling that Gina didn't like her. There was so much tension between the two. "Do I have to go?" she asked.

"Yes you do." Denise wrote down a couple of food items on her list. "Let's see, if you take lunch two days next week, and buy lunch for three days, then I think we will be all right until payday." Denise folded the piece of paper and put it in her wallet behind the fifty-dollar bill.

"I'll just take lunch for the whole week," Nicole said after noticing the crumpled piece of paper in her mother's hand that she knew was a grocery list. "I really don't want to go to Gina's. She looks at me like I'm the bad seed or some other evil thing." Her voice became softer as she spoke and her eyes started misting. "And she is always telling me what I need to do and she goes on and on about how you two used to live the life before I was born. I'm tired of hearing that. She makes me feel like that I have thrown a wrench in her lifestyle and I am not even her child." Nicole began to cry. "Some kind of godmother she is."

"Come here, sweetie." Denise put her arms around her daughter and held her tight. "Everything is going to be all right."

Nicole held on to her mother. "Gina's a witch," she whispered. She hoped her mother didn't hear what she had just said. There was something about Gina that Nicole could not understand. It wasn't that she didn't like Gina, her ways and attitudes toward people were different from other people she knew. She was nervous whenever she was around Gina.

Denise heard her, but pretended not to. Gina did lay the lectures on a little too thick when it came to Nicole. Denise broke the silence. "How about we stay up all night and watch movies?"

Nicole went to the DVD rack, selected a couple of DVD's, and snuggled on the sofa with her mother. They watched movies until they both fell asleep.

*****

Denise woke up the next morning in a good mood, despite the pouring rain. It was so dark outside that she didn't know what time of morning it was. She got up and sat on the edge of the sofa where she fell asleep the night before.

Feeling good was something she liked. She started humming Yolanda Adam's song, *The Battle Is Not Yours*. She was tired of fighting battles, especially the ones she could not win. She finally came to the conclusion that she was never going to look like the women in the magazines that she was always buying. Trying to look and act perfect for a man was no guarantee that she would get one. She figured if beautiful women who were in the entertainment industry with money, looks, and brains had trouble with men being faithful to them, then looks and money were not the issue. Those men just had no morals. She realized what Lita was trying to get through to her all this time. She thought about all of the money she would have had if she had not invested in tons of magazines, zillions of colors of nail polish, make-up, tons of earrings, and self-help books. She would have had a nice little savings.

*****

It was 4:45 in the evening. The circular driveway led to an immaculate yard with perfectly trimmed hedges and numerous rose bushes. There were a couple of birds splattering in the birdbath located in the center of the yard. Denise was happy that Gina could amass this type of lifestyle on her own, but sometimes she felt that the people who really deserved to live like this often got the short end of the stick. She loved Gina dearly, but why couldn't they both live the same way? Denise figured it would have been fair if they both lived the good life and were happy or they both could live the way she is living and both be miserable.

"Are we staying long? I don't feel comfortable in Gina's house." Nicole started rubbing her temples. Whenever Nicole visited Gina's home she made sure to go straight to the sofa. She would sit in that one spot until it was time to go. Gina never said that Nicole shouldn't touch anything in her house, but two years ago, Gina cautioned Nicole about standing too close to the figurine table and to be careful where she sat her cup. After that incident, Nicole decided that at every visit she would sit on the sofa until it was time to go.

"What's wrong with you? And to answer your question, we'll stay until I get ready to go." Denise didn't intend to stay long because she knew how uncomfortable Nicole felt in Gina's home.

Nicole's head started throbbing. Facing Gina always set something off in her. Finally her breathing slowed and she was already at the count of ten. "I'm all right, Mom. Let's get out of the car and go in. I'm sure she will be glad to see us."

Denise reached over into the backseat and grabbed her purse. "Gina's not that bad, she just has a bad way with words."

The door to the two-story, brick house flew open. Gina stood there with her honey blonde hair slightly touching her lavender silk blouse. Her smooth silky eyebrows were dyed the same color as her hair. Her almond colored body was only slightly toned. She had abandoned her workout at the sight of her first muscle. She was afraid if she continued, she might bulk up like Miss Universe. Her diamond earrings with the matching diamond necklace were blinding. The light breeze blew the scent of her perfume through the air. She started walking down the steps to greet her visitors.

"What?" a surprised Nicole asked. "You mean she's coming to us and not waiting for us to come to her."

"Stop it, Nicole." Denise tried to make her fake smile look real. She had a feeling that something wasn't right. Suddenly the good feeling Denise had earlier that morning left her. As she got closer to Gina, she could tell by the look on her face that something was wrong. Even though Gina was dressed well, she still looked bad to Denise. As they got closer to each other, Gina held out her arms to embrace Denise, something she hardly ever did.

Once they got inside, Nicole looked around the living room area. She didn't know where to sit. There was a new sofa against the wall. Denise was standing too. The three of them stood there engaging in small chit-chat. Two minutes had passed and Gina had not offered them a place to sit, and she was still standing also. She noticed the awkward look on her mother's face when she glanced over at her.

"If you want, you two are welcome to sit down," Gina finally said.

If we want, Nicole thought. "I'll stand," Nicole quickly said.

"Sit down." Denise motioned to Nicole. She pointed to the white leather sofa.

"Oh, no, not there," Gina said. She walked to the adjacent dining room and brought a hard dining room chair for Nicole to sit on. She went back and got another one for Denise. Gina stood against the bar area in the living room, near a display of shot glasses she had collected from places she had visited. There were over one hundred glasses on the wall display, mostly from cities in the United States and a few from outside of the country. Gina didn't say anything. She stared at the glasses on the wall as if her mind was going back in time, reminiscing about happier days.

Nicole started tapping her feet on the carpet, trying to make noise on purpose. She looked over at her mother who was now becoming annoyed because of Gina's inattentiveness and semi-rude behavior when dictating where they could and could not sit.

"Gina," Denise said forcefully. "Remember us? Your company?"

Gina didn't answer. She continued looking at the wall while humming an unfamiliar tune.

Nicole snickered and looked down at her hands. She raised her hand to her mouth pretending to bite her nails, while mumbling under her breath, "I knew she was crazy."

Denise looked at Nicole and mouthed the words, *shut the hell up*!

Gina heard her and responded, "I'm not crazy, Nicole. I'm dying."

Chapter 10

Justin was steaming. Heat consumed his whole body. Anger and rage was about to overtake him. Every emotion known to man ran through him. He felt betrayed. Secrets should never be revealed, especially secret relationships. He would never get the chance to see or hold Blair again. Their children would never be born and they would never get to share a home or life together. All of their dreams were just like her—dead. It was all *their* fault. How could *they* do that to him or Blair? She had never hurt anyone, especially *them*. But *they* were the cause of her destruction, her demise, *they* ended her life.

Justin walked back to his dining room and looked at the large brown envelope lying on the table. The postmark on it was November 3, the day after Blair shot herself. He didn't know when it arrived in the mail, because all he did was go to the mailbox, get the mail, and throw it on the table. Today, four months later, he was just getting around to sorting and opening his mail. There was no urgency since his bills and mortgage were debited monthly from his checking accounts. The sympathy cards, flyers, and that large brown envelope sat on his table for months. He would only go to his mailbox when it was so full that it would not close.

Today he decided it was time for him to get his life back together. It had been two weeks since the day he was standing on the sidewalk outside the gym and crossing paths with Carole and Arlene. Nothing bad had come out of the situation. So he figured he was in the clear.

He flashed back to earlier in the morning when he had made up his mind to snap out of his depression and get on with his life. He eased his mind by praying and relaxing in a warm bath and taking in the scents of the aromatherapy candles lit in the living room. That was something Blair taught him to do when he was stressed or needed to clear his head or just simply for relaxation. That quiet hour gave him the motivation he needed to start his healing process.

He had his housekeeper come and clean his home from top to bottom. He gathered his clothes that needed to be sent to the cleaners and got his Jaguar detailed on his way back from dropping off his clothes. He then went to the local day spa for the works. He stepped out with a fresh haircut, shave, full body massage, pedicure, and manicure. He felt like a new man and walking in to a clean, good smelling house made him feel even better.

Justin put in a Sade CD. He wanted to listen to music while he went through his mail. Most of it was junk mail, which he quickly discarded. He finally got to the envelope. There was no return address on it, so he did not know it was from Blair until he opened it up.

He was still staring at the envelope. It explained why Blair killed herself. The note didn't sound like a suicide note, but the contents may as well have been one. Inside were pictures of him and another woman in Miami Beach, an answering machine tape, and a black onyx diamond earring.

He didn't have to wonder how Blair came in to possession of the items. She enclosed a very brief note explaining that the pictures were mailed to her, someone called her house one morning and her answering machine recorded him making love to another woman, and she found the earring rolled in his dirty linen when she was doing his laundry. She had possession of these items for months before she decided to give it all back to Justin. She named all three women and was right on every count.

Justin's world came crashing down again. Now he knew for sure that Blair knew about the other women. He never thought he could hate a woman. But now these three were people whom Justin didn't want to lay eyes on ever again. He eased his mind by making himself believe that he was not the cause of Blair's death. He was very careful when he cheated on her. She would have never known about the other women if they had not left their calling cards. He thought about confronting each of the women. He knew that would not bring Blair back. He decided to keep his distance from the women who caused Blair's death. There was nothing they could do for him and there was nothing that he wanted from them anymore. Their services, as he called it, were no longer needed.

Depression was coming back into Justin's life. It wasn't even gone for a day. He stood in the middle of his big, clean, three-story house. He smelled good and looked good. He looked around at all he had and wondered why he was still alone. He knew why. The one he was supposed to share his love, house, money, and life with was gone. But he still didn't think it was his fault that Blair was not there. He became frustrated and tired of thinking about what could have been and he just stood there until all the flames on his lit candles flickered away.

Chapter 11

Lita was rearranging her large walk-in closet. Some of the clothes she had purchased months ago were still in bags. She had used Justin's card after all. On the night of Blair's death, she told Denise that if she wanted to go home early it would be okay and she would close up the boutique. Denise took her up on the offer. Two minutes after Denise left, Lita was helping herself to Justin's credit card. Justin's doggy dog ways cost him ten thousand dollars worth of merchandise that night, courtesy of Lita. As she bagged her merchandise she thought about Blair. Blair should have taken this card to the limit, if it has one, she thought. Lita figured since she used the card on the same day Blair was in the shop, Justin would never know it was her purchases. Lita already had her mind prepared for prison a long time ago. That's where she said she would go before she let a man make a fool of her again. Theft by credit card didn't scare her at all. So she doubled what Blair had spent on herself that gloomy day.

Lita really didn't care if Justin found out or not. Whatever amount of money Justin was out of was not enough as far as she was concerned. He had money, a nice body, and good looks, but the sight of Justin made her want to hire someone to take him into a dark alley and beat the daylights out of him, just enough to scare him for all of the women he betrayed. He was so predictable, just like all of the men she had come across in the past two years. Lita knew that if a man could get a little on the side and get away with it, he would do it. She recalled whispering to Justin when he was in the boutique to pick up his Visa card. Lita had told him that she was available for him anytime, as she had been on the two previous times they had sex.

Lita had the art of pretending to enjoy sex with men to a tee. But she hated every minute of it. After her last boyfriend betrayed her, something inside of her just died. After that she stopped looking for the good in men and started looking to see what good they were to her in the finance department. The richer they were the better for her. Lita thought it was easier for her to find a man to have sex with and play him for his money than it was for her to find someone she could trust with her heart. Married men and men with girlfriends were her targets. They were the easiest ones to get money from. She called it her hush money. These gullible men figured if they gave women money, the affair would stay secret. Little did they know, it depended on what type of women they were dealing with. Lita learned a long time ago that single men, meaning men without girlfriends, were the cheapest ones around. They were not going to give up a dime of their money. She knew they figured there was no need to. They have no one to report to.

Lita sat on the edge of bed staring into her closet. Her mind kept going back to her old friend Myra. What she did to her would send any woman off. She told herself that doing that once to a woman and not getting sliced up should have been enough, but it wasn't.

She would call Myra from her cell phone, pretending she was on a lunch break while she was on her way to Myra's house to have sex with her husband. This went on for six months until Lita decided it was time for Myra to find out how unfaithful her husband was. It didn't matter that she and Myra weren't going to be friends anymore. Friends were not going to pay her bills.

During one of her weekly "friendly" phone calls to Myra, Lita became jealous while listening to Myra go on about her lovely home, trips to the day spa, trips to beautiful islands, shopping sprees, and only working because she wanted to. She resented her asking why she didn't have a man. Lita had listened to Myra brag as Lita walked to the front door of Myra's home that day. After she replied to Myra about how happy she was for her and she deserves a *good man* like Leonard, Lita said her goodbye and walked straight into Leonard's arms as he stood in the front door.

As Leonard walked up the stairs, Lita followed behind him wishing he would hurry and start what she came there for. He turned and grabbed her before she made it to the bed. She gave him a long, slow kiss, then backed away to remove her jacket. She threw it across the night stand next to the bed, but not before pushing the redial button on her cell phone.

Seeing Blair stretched out on the sidewalk that day had sent chills up Lita's spine. No man was worth ending your life for. She wondered if Blair ever knew the tape was from her. No one knew she and Justin had ever slept together. They always played it off when he came into the boutique. Even though they had only been together twice, it took a lot for them to pretend that they had never been intimate. That's what freaked her out on the day Blair killed herself. She wondered if Blair had put two and two together. Never in a million years did she want Blair to kill herself. Lita just wanted Blair to leave Justin at least until she could get a small fortune out of him, then Justin would be free to go back to Blair.

Justin was an easy target. He came in one evening ten minutes before closing to pick up a blouse that Blair had picked out earlier that day. Lita did her little flirting routine and had him back in the stockroom and butt naked in a matter of five minutes. She went as far as to dig her nails deep in his back to leave evidence of their encounter. She hoped Blair would come across this in their moment of intimacy and leave Justin. She had nothing against Blair, but she wanted the things that Justin could give her. And if she had to give up a little, she had no problem with that. Lita felt that if Justin was going to be a dog, sleep with other women, and still dish out hush money, then why shouldn't she be on the receiving end?

The second time she and Justin were together came to mind. Lita got great satisfaction out of talking Justin into coming in to the boutique early one morning before it opened. She called him on his cell phone and asked him if he would like more of what he got the last time. Justin was so predictable; she knew he would take her up on her offer. Once in the storeroom, Lita walked behind some boxes in the pretense of getting a blanket to put on the floor. She went to her spare cell phone that she had strategically placed so Justin would not see it. Lita knew Blair would be at work and that her answering machine would record everything. She dialed Blair's number that she retrieved from the customer file, went over to Justin, took him by the hand, and led him close to the area where the cell phone was hidden.

Lita made sure that she called out Justin's name often, so that Blair would know for sure it was him on the tape. She knew Justin would never call out her name. Lita recalled asking him on their first sexual rendezvous how he kept from calling Blair by other women's names. Justin told her that during sex with other women, he always called them *baby.* That way he never had another woman's named ingrained in his head. Lita then knew her name would never leave his lips. All Blair would know is that Justin had been with another woman. She felt this would make Blair leave him for sure. She certainly didn't want her dead.

But Lita had this odd feeling that Blair had known something. She kept thinking back to that day. Remembering the last words Blair had said to her made the hair on the back of her neck stand up. She remembered how Blair had looked her dead in the eyes before she walked out of the boutique that day and told her, not Denise, that when she sees

Justin again, tell him to have a happy life.

"Oh my God, she knew." Lita took in a deep breath. "Oh Blair, all I wanted you to do was leave him. Oh God, how did she know I was the woman on her answering machine?" Lita could feel her stomach churning. She started to sweat. She opened her bedroom window to get some air. The guilt that had overtaken her body only lasted a few seconds. Lita's head and heart were too messed up to have lasting pity for anyone. She took a couple of deep breaths and told herself that there was nothing she could do about Blair now. She chose not to worry about it. Worry and guilt did not pay her bills.

She walked over to her bed, sat on the edge, and fell backwards letting her hands land above her head. She stared at the ceiling for a few seconds and then quickly sat up and reached for the laptop that was on her nightstand. She powered it on and went to her favorite website. "This red Coach purse is just what I need," she said as she added it to her cart and hit the checkout button. After Lita made her purchase, she decided to take a drive.

Chapter 12

Carole was taking the last of the night cream off her face. This had been her second week back at the gym after taking a month off. The soreness was finally going away. But the evil looks she kept getting from Arlene were on her mind. She knew Arlene and Justin had been sleeping together. Even though Carole had more men than she could handle at the moment, Justin would be the cream of the crop. Carole knew that some men cherished their money and their immoral ways more than they did their women. That's why she had no problem taking as much money from men as she could get. She got satisfaction out of bilking men for as much money as she could. None of them knew about the others and that's how she wanted to keep it. She surely didn't want to mess that up until she could put together a new group. Carole had found herself some easy, sad men who thought they had found love.

Carole thought back to her first day back at the gym. There had been a lot of women there, but none were her friends. She wasn't an approachable woman. She was too quiet—a dangerous kind of quiet. Everyone did their best to stay out of her way. She didn't care if a woman liked her or not, and it showed. Men were her only concern. There was nothing a woman could do for her, not even be a friend. She felt that women stab your heart deeper than men do.

Carole wrapped her hair and secured it with a scarf. She wanted to forget all of the gym scenes she'd had with Arlene. Her mind went back to Justin and how he had not budged at her recent attempts for sex. It made her wonder if Arlene had that area wrapped up or if he hadn't returned to his *giving* mood yet. She reached for her day planner that was on the foot of her bed. She flipped through it, checking her appointments, hoping she could get her mind off Justin. She thought back to when she had called him a couple of days last week and tried to invite herself over, but he had declined. She thought about calling him now, but he'd made excuses about being busy on her two previous attempts. She had visited him a couple of times since Blair's death, but he was not good company. Justin couldn't even hold a coherent conversation. Anyway, conversation wasn't what Carole wanted. His body and money would do just fine. After their first sexual encounter, Carole made every effort to set up a weekly tryst, but Justin was too committed to Blair, so he said, to ever leave her, even though he cheated whenever he got the opportunity. Knowing that Justin would never leave Blair, Carole decided she had to do something to make

Blair leave him. Carole never thought that leaving the earring in Justin's laundry hamper in the bathroom would lead to Blair's suicide. She knew Blair would find it since Justin told her that she couldn't stay long because Blair was coming over to do laundry and take some clothes to the cleaners later that afternoon. Carole told Justin she understood and didn't want to come between the love of his life.

The clock on her nightstand had 10:45 p.m. *What the hell,* she thought. Carole picked up the phone and dialed Justin's number. She was a little restless and needed something to calm her.

"Hello," Justin said. This was the first time that he had answered his phone all day. Carole had called about four times earlier in the day. She left a message each time telling Justin that she is available whenever he feels like having company. "Hello," he said again.

"Hi, Justin. I just called to see how you are doing," she said cautiously.

Blair's letter that he read days earlier came back to haunt him. Justin was sitting at his desk in his home office wrestling with the anger he had for Carole. Loneliness had been his friend for a long time since Blair's death. Justin reminded himself that there was nothing he could do to bring Blair back, but he still didn't know if he had it in his heart to forgive those manipulative women who tore his life apart. He hadn't been with a woman for months, and figured he deserved a little TLC right now, even if the thought of Carole disgusted him. His hormones won the battle. "I'm doing as well as can be expected. What can I do for you?"

"What do you mean by that?" Carole asked.

Justin's mind was now on sex. At this point, he didn't care who he got it from. "Mean by what?"

"Okay, let's not play games, Justin. You know why I called and want to know if I can come over," she said in a demanding voice.

"What's wrong with you?" Justin let out a sigh like he didn't want to be bothered. He didn't want Carole to know he was just as ready as she was.

"Nothing." Carole was not ready to give up.

Justin's phone clicked. "Someone's on my other line. Why don't you come over? I know that's what you called for," he said.

Carole had a big grin on her face as she was taking the scarf from her hair. "I'm on my way. Bye."

Justin clicked over. It was Lita.

"Hello," Justin said dryly.

"Hi, handsome. I haven't heard from you in a while. What are you doing?" Lita asked.

Justin didn't answer for a few seconds. "Nothing. I'm just sitting here doing some paperwork," he replied. He grabbed a couple of pieces of paper and made crumpling noises.

"Would you like some company? I can stop and pick up something if you're hungry." Lita was hoping he would say skip the food and come right on over.

Justin yawned. "No, it's getting late and it is about time for me to go to bed." He focused on a picture of Blair that was on his desk. "I haven't had much of an appetite lately."

Lita held the phone trying to think of something to say to get him to change his mind. "We haven't really gotten to know each other. Don't get me wrong, the stockroom thing was fun, but let's try for something more comfortable." Lita was trying really hard to be convincing. "Why don't you come and visit me? I understand if you don't want your territory invaded right now." Lita was desperate for money. She had to work her plan fast.

"Two women. Hmmh."

"What?" Lita asked. "Did you just say two women?" She took her cell phone off her ear and removed her earring. She wanted to make sure she was hearing things correctly.

Justin didn't answer her question. "Hey, Lita, where are you?"

"Not too far from your house." *Oh my God,* she thought. *I'm not supposed to know where he lives. I need to say something to throw him off. Maybe he didn't hear me.*

"How do you know where I live?" Justin didn't think much of her saying she knew where he lived, it was just an automatic question.

Lita was a pro. "I don't. I just know what area. Everyone knows you live in Ginger Valley," she said quickly. Lita had been driving around for ten minutes looking for Justin's street. She had never been to his house, but had an idea where Peppermill Street was. She got his information from the customer file at the boutique.

"What about tomorrow night?" he asked. "I need to catch up on some paperwork before I go to sleep," he lied.

"What time and where?" she asked with an attitude. Lita was more than desperate. Her funds from her last conquest were running low and her paycheck from the boutique was just pocket change. She needed money to pay for a two week vacation in Hawaii, and to get a wardrobe, along with paying her rent and other bills while she was away.

Justin was trying to think of something to say. "I'll call and let you know. I have your cell number on my caller ID." Justin glanced at his caller ID to make sure there was an actual number.

Lita let out a silent sigh. "That's fine, Justin, but the stockroom is off limits. I have more class than that. I only did that with you on a whim."

"I guess you got whimmed twice." He laughed. Then he laughed louder, almost uncontrollably. He didn't want to think about Blair. Laughing kept him from crying.

"Oh, I can give you better than what you had," Lita said angrily. "The third time is the charm. Just make sure it is somewhere nice, if we can't meet at your place." She was mad. *How dare he laugh at me*, she thought. "And this is no joke. I am not some slut off the street, if that's what you're thinking. I do have class," she said.

Class, he thought. "You know my reputation," he said in his smooth, sexy voice, which wasn't around two seconds ago. "I only surround myself with the best. Don't worry about where we will be." He chuckled. "I will take care of that. Talk to you tomorrow, baby."

He thinks this is funny and he called me baby. I guess he couldn't think fast enough to call the right woman's name. I remember him telling me that there are only two reasons why men call you baby. One, when they are not emotionally involved with you and call you baby because they can't keep the names of their women straight. Two, when you are the only woman in their life and it is used as a term of endearment and they mean it. His baby applied to the former. "I will be looking forward to your call, but it doesn't mean that I am necessarily sitting by the phone waiting," Lita said. "If you do, you do and if you don't, well then you just don't." She thought about how many women Justin had under his spell with his broken promises and lies. He was in for a big surprise. She figured Justin couldn't play her even if he wanted to. His game just wasn't that tight. "Sweet dreams, baby. Talk to you tomorrow."

Justin pushed the off button on his phone. He knew Lita was gaming and he told himself that he is too smart for that, because he had already run into plenty of women like her. He gave her credit with the cell phone trick. He wondered how many other men Lita had run this game on. He knew that some women were just as bad as men were when it came to relationships. He remembered one woman telling him, after he asked for her phone number, wrote it down, and put it in his wallet, that he should memorize it. He asked her why. She informed him that's how most men get caught. Almost every woman goes through her boyfriend's wallet, glove compartment, cell phone, or pager whenever she gets a chance. Women really don't get caught that way. They have a memory of an elephant. Women memorize phone numbers when they don't want to get caught, then delete the call out of their cell phone when done. He always wondered why some of the women he had given his phone number to would throw the paper away when they thought he wasn't looking. It had to be true, because a couple of days later, he would get a call from these women. They memorized the number before discarding the paper. I guess some women can be cheaters too.

Lita was two blocks from Justin's street approaching a stop sign. She was hoping her eyes were deceiving her. A vehicle zoomed past the four way stop sign going about fifty miles an hour. It didn't bother to stop. The man on the motorcycle skidded and ran into the curb. He was almost hit. Lita parked her Tahoe on the curb and got out to see if the man was all right.

She ran over to where he was. "Hey, mister. Are you okay?" Lita helped him over to the curb to sit down. "Do you need an ambulance?" she asked. She watched him as he tried to catch his breath.

The man got up a little shaken, but he was okay. "No, I'm fine," he said as he brushed the dirt off of his jeans. "Believe it or not, this is not the first time this has happened. A lot of people don't know there is a stop sign at this corner because the street has a sharp curve and it straightens out right when you get to the stop sign." He pointed out the curved street to Lita. "I live just up the street. I'm okay, just glad that I didn't get hit by the damn red Escalade."

Lita saw Carole's vehicle before she saw the guy on the motorcycle. She was so caught off guard that her heart almost stopped. She was wondering what she was doing on her way to Justin's. "I'm glad that you're okay, mister. Maybe your neighborhood needs to get together with the city and do something about this intersection," she said with anger in her voice that was not directed toward the man. Lita walked back to her car and proceeded to leave. She started to call Justin back, but decided against it. He was just being a man. She now knew why Carole frequently questioned her about Justin. Lita became angry that Carole was after a rich, eligible man, when Carole had all the men and money that she could ever need. Lita knew she had to work fast to get her hooks into Justin before Carole found out for sure that she was after Justin and fire her.

Chapter 13

There were so many numbers to memorize. Social security, driver's license, bank accounts, pin number to bank accounts, answering machine code, cell phone numbers, code to check cell phone messages, all of these numbers she had memorized. Arlene knew that no matter how many times people are told not to, they still use part of their birth dates, social security numbers or driver's license numbers as an access code of some sort. Arlene had figured all this out and had them all lined up in her head. She knew everything she needed to know about Justin—how much money he had in the bank, who called, and the times of his appointments. She had not managed to get a copy of his house keys and the code to his alarm yet, but she was working on that. She retrieved the other information by going through his glove compartment and wallet while he was sleeping.

Even though Blair was out of the picture, her plan to snag Justin was moving slower than she expected. She hoped Blair didn't kill herself because of the pictures she sent of her and Justin. This had Justin in such a deep depression that he could not focus on life, let alone a relationship. What really threw a wrench in her plans were Lita and Carole. She had heard the messages that were left on Justin's answering machine, so she knew there was a lot going on between him and those women. She was careful not to delete any messages, just in case he became suspicious.

She thought about calling Justin. The clock read 12:02 a.m. Since it was so late, she thought against it and decided to give him a couple more weeks. She had plenty of time on her hands, so waiting wasn't a problem.

Chapter 14

Lita's mind wasn't focused on work. She had already made her first three customers of the day mad. She over-rang one, gave another the wrong amount in change, and the third customer told Lita she didn't like her attitude. "Do you have this in a size nine?" asked another customer. The woman held up the dress so Lita could see it. After about two seconds, she put her arm down. She threw the dress across a rack and was about to turn around and walk off before Lita answered.

"I'm sorry, so sorry. Let me go check in the back." Lita knew she had to pull herself together. She was beginning to hate her job at the boutique more and more. It was only last night that she had seen Carole go zooming by on her way to Justin's. If she did not need the money she would not have come in.

The woman turned back around and picked up the dress. "A size nine," she yelled as Lita walked to the stockroom.

It took her only thirty seconds to find the dress and bring it out to the woman. "Will you need anything else?" Lita asked. "I apologize for my inattentiveness earlier. I'm here by myself this morning."

The woman held the dress out inspecting it for any imperfections. "No problem. Thanks for finding the dress for me."

"Will that be all?" Lita asked as she walked to the register with the dress in hand.

The woman pulled her wallet out of her purse. "Yes, that will be all, thanks."

Lita was careful to ring up the correct price of the dress and since the woman was paying with a credit card, Lita didn't have to worry about giving her the incorrect change. She made sure to smile this time.

*****

Denise was behind the counter straightening the jewelry display. She greeted the customer who was purchasing a dress, rung up her purchase, and told her to have a good afternoon. Her mind was on Gina. The news of her illness had shaken her up. Her best friend was dying. She was tired of people around her dying. "Oh God, what is going to happen next?"

Lita heard her whispered question as she walked behind the counter. "Maybe the sky will fall in." Lita sat down on a chair near the register after her customers left. She really didn't feel like working. She wasn't sick, just frustrated and annoyed that Carole was trying to get her hooks into Justin. "What were you just saying?"

Denise stared at Lita wondering about her sarcastic remark about the sky falling in. "I was talking to myself," Denise said. She took a deep breath to keep from saying something just as silly as Lita. "Do you remember my friend Gina?"

Lita couldn't get her mind off of Justin and Carole. Her head started spinning. The thought of Carole getting her hands on more money made her angry and the thought of working in Carole's boutique made her ill. "Yes," she said, answering Denise's question. "And you have been talking to yourself a lot lately."

"What?" Denise asked as if she had not quite heard Lita.

"Talking to yourself," Lita replied.

Denise folded her arms and had to think a second. She realized that Lita was mixing conversations. She decided to go with the conversation of her talking to herself. She sighed. "I guess it's just an unconscious habit because I don't realize it until after it's done."

"Can you get help for that?" Lita asked jokingly.

"Oh, so you think I'm crazy?" Denise went back to arranging the jewelry in the display cabinet. She looked over at Lita and shook her head while thinking she was the one who needed to get help for her money stealing addiction.

"No, I didn't say you were crazy. You just talk to yourself too much and I don't mean every once in a while. You do it every single day." Lita slid down in the chair appearing exhausted.

"I guess you're Miss Perfect. At least I'm not running after men trying to punk them for their money." Denise locked the jewelry case and walked to the dressing room to collect clothes that were left behind.

"Whatever." Lita was not in the mood for an argument with Denise. It wasn't worth it. If she lost the argument, she would get nothing out of it. If she won, she still would get nothing out of it. So why bother? Lita learned a long time ago not to waste her time and energy on anything that had no benefit for her. "You know, I'm not feeling very well. I'm going home." Lita got up, grabbed her purse from behind the counter, and proceeded out the door.

"Bye," Denise said. "And I was talking to you this time." There was humiliation in her voice. She stood there for a moment wondering if it was normal to do that.

Lita opened the door and came back in. "Look, Denise, forget I said anything. I really didn't mean it. I have a lot on my mind. If I feel better later on, I will come back to help you. Call me if you need me." Lita went back behind the counter to get her umbrella. She looked at Denise with apologetic eyes. She really liked Denise and had nothing against her. The thought of Carole and Justin together last night had just gotten under her skin. "And I did hear you when you mentioned Gina. We can talk about it later if you want. I just need to get out of here right now."

"I hope you feel better," Denise yelled to Lita as she went out the door. "I know she didn't mean anything by it," she said to herself. "Why do I keep doing that? I do talk to myself."

Out on the sidewalk, Lita took a few steps toward her SUV. She was trying to decide where to go. She hadn't felt like working and she surely didn't want to go home. *There's got to be something better than this. I am really tired. I have nothing to look forward to.* She opened her vehicle door and sat in her seat staring at the steering wheel. A piece of paper on her windshield caught her attention. "I wish people would stop putting things on my windshield," she said out loud. She got out of her vehicle and snatched the folded paper from under the windshield wiper. She got back in and threw the paper on the seat. *Where can I go?* she thought. She started her engine and looked at the gas gauge. "Can't go too far," she said. "Truck is almost on empty." She looked over at the passenger seat and saw the paper she had taken off the windshield. She picked it up and opened it. She read it and almost stopped breathing when she got to the end of the note. She looked around to see if the person who had put it there was still around, but she knew better. No one in his or her right mind would stand around to be noticed. The letter read:

I saw you creeping through the neighborhood last night.

What neighborhood? she thought. She drove through a lot of neighborhoods last night. She recalled driving around Justin's neighborhood. Carole immediately came to mind. It had to be her. She wondered why Carole would leave a note instead of telling her face to face that she saw her. She thought about it for a while longer and decided that right now she didn't care if Carole saw her or not. Lita folded the paper and stuffed it in her purse.

Denise looked out the window of the boutique. She saw Lita sitting in her vehicle. Denise knew that Lita was tired of working because Lita told her a couple of weeks ago that she was about to put her plan into motion. She noticed that Lita hadn't started her vehicle yet. She saw her reading something and then looking around as if she was waiting for someone. She watched her as she looked in her rear view mirror for about five seconds. Lita then placed both of her hands on the steering wheel and laid her head on her hands. She thought Lita was thinking about her next move as she lifted her head, started her vehicle, and pulled away from the curb.

Denise was thankful for her two jobs. Her job at the bank was enough to pay all of her bills, but she didn't have much left over. She was glad she was able to get this part-time job at the boutique. She still wasn't able to put enough away for a decent savings, but she still had just enough to make it from payday to payday. One thing for sure, she knew she couldn't and didn't want to do what most of her friend's and what Lita was doing. She didn't have it in her to go after men for their money. It wasn't right and it was too much work. Now she understood what Lita meant when she said she had two jobs. She has seen Lita's "to do" list on how to get money from men. Lita was right. It is a job.

*****

Lita sat quietly in the dimly lit room. She knew this place was just as good as the gym to relieve stress. There weren't many people inside since it was still early. The slow music and the light aroma helped her to relax. The waitress sat the cup of herb tea on the table next to the candle. Lita had told her what she wanted when the waitress greeted her at the door and led her to her table. She cupped both hands around the teacup. The warmth took away some of the chill that she felt. She was trying not to lose control. Things weren't going as fast as she planned. The economy was bad, and she realized that men weren't as free with their money as they had been in the past. Lita leaned back in the chair, closed her eyes, and thought back to another past boyfriend, another cheater.

The aroma of the tea made Lita open her eyes and take a sip. Painful memories and bad relationships came back to haunt her. She really tried not to think about what the men in her relationships had done to her. Looking or waiting for a decent man to come into her life was useless. All she knew to do now is to get with a man, get all she could out of him, and go on to the next man. She closed her eyes again and told herself to stop thinking about the past. The future is what she needed to concentrate on. She closed her eyes again.

"Wake up, girl."

Lita quickly opened her eyes. Startled, she almost knocked over the cup of tea. The way things had been going for her lately, she didn't need anyone sneaking up on her. As soon as her heart rate resumed its normal beat, she replied. "I wasn't asleep. I was just relaxing. What are you doing here anyway?"

"I went by the boutique to see you and you were pulling off as I was pulling up. I saw you come here, but I had to stop at the gas station across the street." Justin pulled up a chair and sat down. "What kind of place is this?"

"It's a relaxation tea room." Lita caught the waitress's attention. The flame had gone out on the candle and she wanted it re-lit. She was agitated that Justin had come along and invaded her space. She wasn't feeling him right now. "Why were you looking for me?"

"Why is it so dark in here?" Justin took the lighter from the waitress and re-lit the candle. "We have a date tonight," he said while winking his eye at the waitress.

"It's not night yet." Lita stared him straight in his eyes when he turned to look at her. *He just couldn't wait. It has been less than twenty-four hours since he has been with Carole. He's the kind of man that gets any woman he wants when he wants them. He goes through women like it's nothing. I hate him.*

"I know that. I have a couple of things to do. I just wanted to let you know where to meet me. First I thought we could have drinks at Dalveaux's Sports Bar and then dinner at Montague Place." Justin returned the stare.

Lita leaned in closer to the table. "Then what?"

Justin moved in closer. "Let's just say, it will be a surprise. It will be a night you'll never forget.

"So I guess you're going to put it on me?" Lita wanted money from a man, and nothing else. But she knew she had to give them what they wanted in order for her to get what she wanted.

"I have skills, baby. Eight o'clock. Don't be late." Justin stood half-way up, and then sat back down. He placed both elbows on the table and interlocked his fingers. He looked Lita in the eyes. "What do you want with me?" Instead of waiting for an answer, he quickly winked his eye at her this time before getting up again. He pulled his wallet from his pocket and took out a fifty dollar bill. He laid it on the table to pay for Lita's tea, which only cost $3.75. "See you tonight."

Lita was glad he left because she had no intention of answering his question. She looked over at the bill on the table. *Now that's what I like.* She picked up the bill, put it in her purse, took out a five, laid it on the table, and left after getting the rest of her tea to go. She caught a glimpse of a woman staring at her as she walked out the door. Lita thought nothing of it. She just blew her off as an envious woman with nothing else to do.

*****

Carole had been at the boutique for about an hour. The fifty percent off sale had brought in a lot more people. Most of the racks were almost bare. The line was nearly out the door. Denise was handling the customers as fast as she could. Carole pitched in to help and she was mad that she had to do so. She is an owner, not a worker. Carole looked at her watch. "How long did you say Lita had been gone?"

Denise looked up for a split second in between scanning merchandise. "About an hour and a half. I don't think she is coming back. She wasn't feeling well." As much as Denise hated being left alone in the boutique, she didn't want to get Lita in trouble.

Carole had called Lita's home twice, but got no answer and she didn't have her new cell number. "Well, if she is sick, she should have been at home by now."

Denise didn't look up this time. "Maybe she went to the doctor." She wanted to run in the back and call Lita on her cell phone and warn her, but there was no way she could leave the counter. Lita was on her own this time. Denise had bailed her out with Carole too many times before.

"Well, what do you know?" Carole saw Lita walking up the sidewalk toward the boutique. "She doesn't look sick to me."

Denise kept working. "Damn," she said. "Here we go."

Lita had a different attitude from this morning. Since she was going to see Justin tonight, she was ready to put her plan in motion. She had bills that needed to be paid and other luxuries that she had gotten used to over the last two years.

As soon as she opened the door to the boutique, Carole ran from behind the counter and lit in on her.

"Who in the hell do you think you are? Do you think you can come and go as you please? You don't own this shop, I do," Carole yelled. "You work the hours that you are scheduled and if you're sick and can't make it in, call me, not Denise. I'm the boss. If I'm not available, keep calling until you get me." Carole paused to catch her breath. "And just for the record, write down how long you were gone today so I can . . ." Before she could finish her sentence she could feel herself stumbling against the wall and her face stinging. It happened so fast that she never saw it coming. Lita had thrown the cup of tea that she had in her hand into Carole's face.

Lita pretended it was an accident. "I am so sorry, Carole. Someone bumped into me and my arm went up and tea flew out of my cup."

"You did that on purpose," Carole yelled.

One woman who saw the whole thing from beginning to end tried to control the big grin she had on her face. "It was an accident. She did trip. I saw it." She turned around so Carole wouldn't see the expression on her face. From her view, it did look like an accident. "No professionalism at all," said the woman as she hung her two dresses across the nearest rack and walked out. "Bosses shouldn't reprimand an employee in front of other people, especially in front of customers." She made sure Carole heard her as the door to the boutique closed.

The embarrassment was almost too much for Carole to bear. She already knew she wasn't good at fighting, so hitting Lita was out of the question, but she sure wanted to. She knew the warm tea thrown at her was intentional, but to save face she went with the accident act that Lita was putting on. She pulled the bottom of her blouse from out of her skirt and wiped her face with it.

Lita had quickly disappeared for a few seconds and came back with wet paper towels. "Are you okay? I am so sorry," she said. "Here, let me help you."

Carole snatched the towels from her and wiped the wetness from her forehead and her hairline. "You know what, Lita," she hissed. "This was no accident and we both know it. You won't get another chance to mess up or humiliate me again."

"Humiliate you? You just stood here two minutes ago and scolded me like I was a two year old in front of a shop full of people." Lita folded her arms in front of her and gave her a "you won't get another chance to do it again" look.

Carole continued wiping her face with the towels. "Oh, but you defended yourself by throwing a cup of tea in my face."

Lita smiled. "I told you that was an accident, sweetheart. Oh and about firing me, you wouldn't do that on the spot. Let's see, you really need four people to run this shop. I have to admit you do have a profitable business. But we both know you are trying to run it with the least amount of employees that you can. It keeps more money in your pocket. So unless you have someone else lined up that doesn't need to be trained to do my job, or who won't steal merchandise and money right under your nose, I think I am pretty safe for a while."

"You are not indispensable, Lita. You can be replaced and you can't always get what you want, and you can't and won't come and go here as you please. Like I said earlier, the boutique is called Carole's, not Lita's." She walked over to the rack of silk blouses and chose a white one to replace the tea stained one she was about to take off. She stood right there in the middle of the room and changed blouses without blinking an eye. "And by the way, you are fired. Now get out of here. Now!" she yelled.

Lita wasn't surprised. She probably would have done the same thing. "I know the name of the boutique. I couldn't care less what it's called. You can have a whole string of boutiques. I don't give a damn. Work is work whether you work at someone else's business or run your own. I don't plan on working for the rest of my life."

"Oh yeah, I forgot, sugar daddies and other women's husbands are more your style."

Lita picked up the Styrofoam cup and walked over to the wastebasket. "You got that right." She caught a glimpse of a woman staring into the window. It was the same woman from the relaxation room. It was a familiar face but she didn't know who the woman was. She had seen her around different places, but couldn't pinpoint where.

Arlene saw the whole tea incident before it even started. She had been following Justin since that morning. She saw him at Serenity Tea Relaxation Room with Lita just a few minutes ago and she saw Carole leave his house at 5:15 a.m. That did not sit well with her. She wanted Justin so bad that it was making her work her plan differently with him than she did with the other three husbands whom she hooked years ago. She didn't love Justin, but wanted him badly as a husband. She divorced her other two husbands after her interest in them declined, and one divorced her. Justin was adventurous, well-mannered, charming, and a dog just like her previous husbands.

Carole saw Arlene gazing into the boutique through the glass door. She opened the door of the boutique as she buttoned the last button on her blouse. "Are you window shopping or spying?"

"When does what I do matter to you?" Arlene walked into the boutique. "Coffee looks good on you. Don't you think you should have been drinking it instead of wearing it?"

"It was tea, you idiot, and when does what I drink matter to you?" she said sarcastically.

“Nothing you do matters to me.” Arlene looked at her watch. “I’ve got to go. You look like you need to get some rest. Looks like you have been up all night.”

“I have and it was worth it.” Carole smiled as she thought about her night with Justin. “And who in the hell are you to be worried about what I need to do?”

“I’m not worried, just making a comment.” Arlene put on her shades, took a deep breath while running her hands through her hair. She lifted her shades slightly off her nose and looked around the boutique. She was impressed. The set up was very nice and well-coordinated. All of the hanging merchandise on the racks was evenly spaced with signage clearly stating the price of the clothing. Expensive looking shoes were displayed neatly against the back wall. There was track blue lighting along the back ceiling which gave the boutique a classy ambiance. The check-out counter was black marble and there was a sunken waiting area near the front entrance of the boutique. “I’ll let you get back to work.” She lowered her shades, turned, and walked out of the boutique.

Chapter 15

"So what do you want to do?" That question left a sinking feeling in the pit of Denise's stomach. She waited for the answer as she dabbed the tears from her eyes. She rested her chin on her right hand as she clung tightly to the tissue. "I just want things to be right," she paused, "and uncomplicated." She thought about asking the question again. She knew she didn't want to know the answer, but in reality, she really needed to know.

Gina was lying across her bed sobbing. "I don't know about anything anymore. I've known for three months about the cancer and I kept it to myself until I told you last week. I had to get my mind, heart, and soul together. I've been going to church for the last two months." Gina set up on the edge of the sofa. "I bet you didn't know that?"

Denise sat up straight in the chair and crossed her legs. She stared at the pictures on the wall. "No I didn't, but that's a good thing that you're going to church."

"I've prayed to God to help me accept his will." Gina sobbed.

Denise's eyes started to mist again. "You didn't ask to be healed?"

Gina wiped the tears from her eyes with her bare hands. "I've learned to accept what I cannot change. If it's God's will that I die, well then I'll have to accept it. Everyone has to leave this earth and no one is ready to go when it's their time to go."

"So, are you saying that you don't want to be healed?" Denise scooted to the edge of her seat and placed her elbows on her knees. She rested her chin in both of her hands. Her mind went back to the time when she kept getting abnormal pap smear results.

"You know, Denise, you always say that I say stupid things when I don't think before I speak." Gina's voice became weak. "Now why would you ask me a stupid question like that? Of course I want to be healed."

Denise sat up straight. "Then you need to be specific in your prayers and ask to be healed." She closed her eyes and after a few seconds opened them and let out a deep breath. "So what are you going to do?" She asked the question with force this time.

"I don't know yet!" Gina's yelling released the tension that had built up in her body. She had been holding everything in so long that she felt heavy with guilt and grief. The release lightened her. "I missed my doctor's appointment last week. I haven't rescheduled. I can't take the thought of being told that the cancer is spreading. I don't know exactly how much time I have and I don't want to know."

Denise let out a deep breath and closed her eyes again. "But still,

Gina, and I don't mean to sound unsympathetic, you still have to get your affairs in order." With her eyes still closed, she leaned over and placed her head against the back of the chair.

Gina felt a sharp pain go through her stomach. She placed her hand on her stomach until the pain subsided. "Whatever I don't get done today just won't get done and trust me, I won't worry about it." Gina looked up at her with swollen eyes. "This will be the last time that I cry over this."

"There's nothing wrong with crying," Denise said. "All I need to know is your decision about your dilemma; the one you're trying to ignore."

"My life is over with, Denise. There is no use in crying anymore. It won't change anything." Gina looked at Denise. "You know what I mean? No more good times for me. It's all downhill now."

"I don't mean to sound cruel, but you haven't had a bad life. And why are you avoiding the question?" Denise asked. She walked over to Gina's wall and viewed the expensive items she had displayed.

"Compared to whose life?" Gina's voice was now filled with a little anger. "Yours? Oh, that's right. Nothing really good has come your way. You have been the good girl all your life and the payoff wasn't what you thought it would be. Bad girls like me got all the luck. Is that what you're trying to say? I guess you're glad that my luck has finally run out."

Denise was still looking at the walls that were covered with pictures and shelves filled with souvenirs of all the places Gina had traveled. She used to think that all those things that Gina had accumulated showed how successful she was, but in fact Gina had been miserable almost all of her life. She had fooled a lot of people. Denise had been fooled most of the time, but now she started to see life more clearly. "Luck. Luck has nothing to do with how people's lives turn out."

"Well for now, luck is on your side," Gina said. "You're not the one who is dying."

"I am dying. You just said so yourself. Everyone has to go, they just don't know when. I could go before you. Someone once told me that every day you wake up, you're closer to death." Denise finally shifted her focus from the wall to Gina's face. "You really know what's important to a person by what they have on the walls of their home. I see expensive art on your wall, shot glasses on the shelves of various places you have visited. But I see that you don't even consider yourself as important."

"I am important to me. I value myself!" Gina folded her arms and closed her eyes. Everything she wanted to do, she hadn't done, even though she had lived a life that some people would kill for. Still it wasn't enough for her. She was always looking for something more than what she already had.

"I don't see one picture of you or any of your family on the wall. You even have a picture of cocaine Eddie in the corner over there." Denise walked over and took a closer look. "I hadn't noticed it before today. I should have known that it's a recent picture. Look at him standing in front of Dalveaux's Sports Bar. Didn't it just opened a couple of weeks ago?" Denise looked back at Gina. "Are you seeing him again?"

Gina looked away and didn't answer. She had started seeing Eddie again three months ago after a three year hiatus. There was chemistry between them that they couldn't ignore. It wasn't lust and it surely wasn't love. It was something that kept them coming back to each other. Whatever she needed, he got it for her. Whether it was a big bank roll, clothes, jewelry, or a bag of weed, Eddie got it for her. But that was back in the day when she was young and wild. She and Eddie had matured and didn't indulge in the crazy lifestyle of their early days. Eddie had been down on his luck in the last couple of years. Gina felt like she owed him because he had been there for her. She felt compelled to help him whenever he asked for it. As time progressed they found out they still couldn't stay away from each other.

"Why do you keep going back to him? Don't answer that, because no matter what I say you're going to do what you want to do anyway, and I've heard all the excuses you have for him to last me a lifetime." Denise slapped Eddie's picture off the wall. She remembered the time he came on to her at Gina's apartment back in the day. When she told Gina about it, she just laughed it off and said it must have been the marijuana he had been smoking and that he probably didn't mean anything by it.

"Why in the hell did you do that?" Before Gina could pick it up off the floor, Denise jumped in front of her.

"I asked you what you plan on doing earlier and you have yet to answer me. And by the way, you don't have a single picture of your goddaughter on the wall. No wonder she hates coming here. You make her feel so uncomfortable."

"You put pictures on your wall of her, she's your daughter. I agreed to be godmother because you are my best friend." Gina didn't have time for children, that's why she did all that she could to make sure she would not become someone's mother. Self-indulgence was what she was good at. Whatever she wanted, she got it by any means necessary.

"Best friend my ass, you did it out of guilt. Your conscious wouldn't let you say no. Your heart really wasn't in it. You didn't give a damn about her when she was born and you still don't." Denise tried not to think about the past and how quickly she had to make the decisions she did regarding Nicole. It was a hard decision and it changed her life. But she didn't regret it, but knew it wasn't too late for some things to no longer remain a secret.

Gina started yelling. "Stop it! Stop it! Don't do this to me!" She walked over to a journal that was on the coffee table, picked it up, and started thumbing through the pages. She quickly flipped through the end, closed it, and threw it back on the table. She looked around as if she was trying to find some misplaced object. She spotted a tablet on the seat of a chair near her dining table. She walked over and picked it up. The envelope she was looking for was sticking out. She took the envelope out and held it in her hand for a while. She fanned herself with it, looked at it again, and stuck it back in the tablet.

"Do what, Gina? Everything came easy to you. Everything," she yelled. "There was always someone around to bail you out or help you along. I'm not coming to the rescue again. Now if you need me to help you through this illness, I'll be there for you. But when it comes to lying, withholding, or padding information for your benefit, I won't do it, anymore." Denise put her hands on top of her head in anger. "And don't jerk me around about what your decision is going to be. If I don't hear from you by tomorrow evening, I will do what I need to do." Denise kicked Eddie's picture from under her foot and walked out the door.

Gina sat on the sofa of her living room staring at the wall for half an hour after Denise left. It took her only thirty minutes to reflect on her life from when she could first remember it up until now. Her life mostly consisted of herself, what she could get, and where she could go. There weren't many people who filled in the "between" parts, just her. As she looked at her expensive art, shot glasses, furniture, and crystal, she realized that none of that was important anymore. She now wondered what was worse, dying from cancer or giving the envelope to Nicole that contained a letter explaining why she gave her away.

Chapter 16

The two hands made a loud clap sound as the two men greeted each other with the classic male handshake. Dalveaux's Sport's Bar was the new hotspot in town. "What's going on, man? Glad to see you out and about again," Leonard said. They had both been recuperating from the loss of their loved one. Myra had left Leonard six months after his tryst with Lita and the cell phone incident.

Justin pulled up a chair and sat with his back towards the table so he could see the comings and goings of the establishment. He liked to see who entered and who left with whom. The eye candy was looking very tempting. "What the hell have you been up to, man?" Justin asked Leonard.

The waitress with a low cut blouse and short black mini skirt distracted Leonard. It took him a couple of minutes to answer as he focused his attention back to the conversation. "Not a damn thing." He started to motion for her to stop by the table on her way back to the bar, then changed his mind when he remembered how empty his bank account was. "Not a damn thing," he said again. "Just getting used to living the single life."

"Me too. Damn she looks good." Justin was staring at the same waitress. "What brings you back to town?"

"Man, I was ordered to come back. Divorce papers that need to be signed. Myra and I have finally come to an agreement about our money, property, and who gets what." His fingers were opening and closing a matchbook that he retrieved from the table. He didn't know why he couldn't stop lying and cheating on Myra. She had been a very good wife. He did and said everything he could think of to get her back into his life.

Justin's eyes were red. He'd had a few drinks while waiting for Leonard to arrive. At least Leonard could see Myra again. Blair was gone for good. "Is Myra taking you to the cleaners?" Justin asked.

"You could say that." He paused. "It doesn't matter. She deserves ten times more than what she's getting for what I put her through. I lied to her so much that I started believing my damn self." Leonard tapped his fingers on the table. "It was a mistake. I made a huge mistake. It killed me to admit to Myra that I had been cheating on her. But I knew I couldn't lie to her anymore. You should have seen the look on her face when she confronted me. The look she had scared the hell out of me. She was too damn calm. I was praying for her to get angry, to call me all kinds of names, to throw something at me, to demand that I do whatever to keep her. But she had that look that all men who are in love with the one they hurt know. It's the one that no man wants to see. It's the look of it's over."

"Man up," Justin said. "They always come back."

"For your ass they do." Leonard wiped his aching eyes. "I would have given anything for her to torture the hell out of me than to leave me." His voice got lower as he struggled to continue. "I know she's not coming back. She's been gone for too long. She's not coming back," he whispered.

Justin looked at Leonard while rubbing his chin. "I wonder why we do this."

"Because we think we will never get caught," Leonard said. "We have learned to always have an airtight story, tell it with tears flowing down our cheeks while we are down on one knee and praying to God that it sounds believable."

Justin sighed and leaned back in his chair. "Well, I would have gotten away with it if it hadn't been for a couple of spiteful women." Justin slammed his fist on the table. It startled Leonard. "Those bitches made sure Blair found out about me." The frown lines in his forehead were deep. He looked mad. "It didn't do them any good. It was a wasted effort on their part." He pulled his chair back and crossed his legs. "They still don't have me and never will."

Leonard didn't want to get pulled into Justin's superior atmosphere. "Well, as I see it, we need to change our ways when we do get lucky and get away with it. But we get up, get dressed, and walk out the door to do it all over again, thinking we will never get caught. And if we do, our woman loves us so much that she will gives us one more chance." Leonard gulped down the tequila shot the waitress sat on the table. "But some women can be so damned evil," Leonard said.

"Oh, now you see what I am talking about," Justin said.

Leonard motioned for the waitress to bring him another shot of Tequila. "That bitch that broke up my marriage didn't have to tell my wife about my business." Leonard held up his index finger to make a point. "But I have realized if I hadn't cheated, there would be nothing to tell. I was wrong for cheating, but she was just as wrong for telling and like you said earlier, what was the point? It didn't get her anywhere or anything that she thought she was going to get."

"You're right, man. She was wrong for that," Justin said. He still didn't get the point that Leonard was trying to make, that the man shouldn't be blameless.

"Myra hates me so much that it doesn't matter what I do or say, she won't take me back. Because God knows I've tried. She has changed all of her numbers. The last time I spoke with her, she told me to talk to a counselor because she couldn't help me."

"Sometimes the woman isn't around to give you that one more chance or to even deny it to you." Justin pulled out his wallet and opened it up to a picture of Blair.

Leonard leaned over to take a look. "She was beautiful. I am so sorry," Leonard said with deep regret.

Justin couldn't take the pain of just looking at the photograph. He wished he could see her in person just one more time. He closed the wallet and put it back in his blazer pocket. "She was my heart. I just hate myself for not making the most of the time that I had with her."

The waitress came back a third time but this time she sat two martinis on the table. "We didn't order this," Justin said.

"Compliments from the woman at the bar," the waitress said.

Leonard quickly grabbed the glass, thanked the waitress, took a sip, and turned toward the bar with a wide grin on his face, which quickly disappeared. "Shit." He turned back around and debated if he should swallow the drink he already had in his mouth or spit it out. He went ahead and swallowed it.

Justin glanced over his shoulder and saw the woman approaching. He smiled. "Right on time." He stood up and pulled out a chair and seated the woman.

"I'm always on time." Lita looked over at Leonard who looked like he was about to pass out. His face was pale and he was slightly trembling. He then became angered and agitated.

"I apologize." Justin gulped down his martini and turned toward Leonard. "Leonard this is Lita." Before he could finish the introductions, Leonard was already on his feet and pushing his chair under the table. He took out a twenty and slammed it on the table.

"No introductions needed. I already know this hater." He took a rigid stance as he glared at Lita. "You disgust me. I was hoping to never lay eyes on you again." His cold steel eyes were glued to her face. They were burning with hate. His fists were balled tight and the muscles in his jaw were tense. He tried in desperation to slow his rapid breathing. Finally, his fast heartbeat slowed.

"Hater?" Justin looked puzzled. He saw the look of disgust on Leonard's face. He turned to look back at Lita who was looking at Leonard with raised eyebrows. His intimidating looks had no effect on her. She was cold-hearted and unshakeable.

"Yeah man, hater. Where have you been in the last year? They're everywhere, gold-diggers with a mission. They are either haters or chasers." Leonard looked at Lita long and hard. Neither would look away nor change the intense look of hate on their faces. Leonard's eyes started burning and he realized that his hands had become two clenched fists. He was desperately trying to keep his arms at his side. He quickly pushed his way past her toward the door. His eyes were stinging. He had lost Myra because of a no good woman who happened to be Lita. He hated her. Leonard knew it was wrong for him to cheat on Myra, but his days were long and boring. Myra was a people person and he was more of a homebody. From the moment Myra brought Lita by the house to show it off, he knew the look he was getting from Lita was more than hello, glad to meet you. It was more of a, "I can't wait to get you to myself" look. His lonely days of working in his home office had finally gotten to him. Lita started doing her so called innocent drop-bys in the middle of the day, knowing Myra wouldn't be home. He remembered the last time he was with Lita. Leonard turned around as Lita was saying, "Focus your attention." When he faced her she had already unzipped her dress that was now on the floor around her ankles. She slowly stepped over the dress revealing the four inch red heels she had on. Focus he did! But he still didn't blame himself for not discouraging her. He convinced himself that if Myra had paid more attention to him, he wouldn't have taken Lita's bait. He now realized having a little of Myra was better than having no Myra at all.

"Wait here," Justin told Lita as he rushed behind Leonard. "Hey man, hold up. What's going on?" Justin maneuvered his way through the crowded club.

Leonard finally made it outside and was pacing up and down the sidewalk with Justin patterning his every move. "That bitch broke up my marriage." The words flowed from his lips.

"Lita? You told me the woman's name was Carlita."

Leonard looked at Justin as if he should have put the name Lita and Carlita together and figured out it was the same person. "Lita, Carlita, whatever she calls herself, she is one in the same." He put his hand on his friend's shoulder. "Sorry man, you couldn't have known. It wouldn't have dawned on me either to put the two names together," he said, trying to help Justin get the look of stupidity off his face.

"That's all right." At the moment Justin realized that he should have known. Getting to really know a woman was the last thing on his mind when he was trying to get her into the bed "Are you going to be okay, man?" Justin looked towards the entrance to make sure Lita hadn't decided to come out and start a scene.

"I will be, but you had better be careful. She's money hungry man. She doesn't care about you or any other man. She told me that from her own mouth after she broke Myra and me up and I wouldn't get with her." Leonard felt his back pocket for his wallet.

"Man, really, I didn't know she was the same broad that broke up your marriage."

"I lost my wife because of her." Leonard pulled out his wallet and put it in his side pocket. "Just making sure she's not a pick-pocket. I don't know what other skills she may have." Leonard walked toward his car while Justin followed him.

"Skills? You act like she takes classes on how to scheme men," Justin said as he and Leonard strolled slowly through the parking lot.

Leonard leaned against his car. "It's her job, man. That's how she survives. She says she chases a man until she can't get anything else out of him, then she's on to the next one. She doesn't care who she hurts and she means it. The last time I saw Carlita, she told me that I couldn't even sex her the right way. She told me she didn't feel a thing." Leonard looked down at the front of her pants. "Lying bitch."

Justin chucked but only for a second. "Man, I wouldn't worry about that. No matter how good a man is in bed, some woman who couldn't get her way with a man has thrown that ego killer line at him some point in his life." Justin let out a sigh. "It has happened to me a couple of times. Even though I knew it wasn't true, it hurt like hell to hear that coming from a woman." Justin was trying not to look down at the front of his own pants, but his eyes made their way down anyway. It was like he was checking to make sure a bulge of some sort was visible.

"Yeah man, that stuff messes with your head. It was a while before I recovered and got my self-confidence back. I'm all right now. It just took me a while to figure out what she was doing." Leonard pulled his keys from his pocket. "Man, I'm telling you, be careful. She is a dangerous woman." He pushed the unlock button on his keychain to unlock his car. "I'm gone man. I have to get out of here." Leonard jumped in the car and drove off.

Justin stood on the curb thinking about how he should have put the two names together. He remembered Leonard telling him about Carlita and how she dialed Myra's work number from her cell phone and left it on while they were getting busy. She had done the same thing to him with Blair. His nostrils started to flair and his breathing became quick. He stood out on the sidewalk and got his composure together before he went back into the sports bar. He was going to let Lita *think* she was playing him. When he finished with her that would end her hating for good. Now he knew what a hater was. His next task was to figure out what category Arlene and Carole fit into. He knew they were trying to run the same game. He had to figure out if they were hating or chasing. It didn't matter because he was not about to be played.

Lita was still sitting at the table sipping her drink and listening to the music as she swayed back and forth to the beat. She looked up and saw Justin emerging from the crowd. She already knew that Leonard had filled him in on their torrid past. She didn't care because she figured Justin didn't care. He was just like her, except he was a man.

Everything he did was for himself. If he had loved Blair so much, he would have kept his dick at home where it belonged. The only difference between them is that she had all the sex she needed. There were plenty of men around for that, but those men didn't have the type of money that she needed. Justin had all the money he needed. He just could not stay with one woman. He needed women and lots of them, just as she needed lots of money. "Is everything okay?" she yelled over the music as Justin neared the table. She looked around and noticed that Leonard had not come back in. "Where is your friend?" She ran her index finger across her lips while looking seductively at Justin.

Justin signaled to the waitress that he wanted to order another drink. He pulled out his chair and sat down. "He left. He had a date." Justin was staring her straight in her eyes.

"Oh really?" She noticed how Justin was trying to intimidate her with his cold, staring eyes. She wasn't frightened one bit.

"Yes, really," he replied.

"Who is Leonard dating now?" Lita asked. "I know he has someone in his life. That man has a healthy appetite for sex." She licked her lips. "He used to wear me out!"

"Why is it so important to you? Do you plan on breaking up another relationship of his? He told me about your little stunt with the cell phone, Carlita."

Lita looked unfazed. "So." Her tone was uncaring.

"So?" Justin said. "Is that all you have to say after what you did to that man's marriage?"

"Blame me. It was all my fault that he was cheating on his wife. I guess he thinks he was the victim," Lita said. "Tell him to get over it. He was the one who messed up."

"He is the victim." Justin leaned across the table toward Lita. "I guess you think you are? His wife left him. Damn. The man is miserable."

"Let me ask you something, Justin." Lita pushed her chair closer in. "Why do men who cheat think they are the victim when they get caught and their wives leave with everything?"

"They are victims when women blackmail them or threaten to tell the wives if things don't go their way." Justin hadn't taken his eyes off Lita since he came back into the sports bar. "You're no good, Lita." He repositioned himself in his chair. "You're no damn good and you're evil."

Lita knew she was no longer a woman with a sensitive soul. Men had drained all the goodness out of her. It didn't matter what name a man called her. She just didn't care anymore. Being a lady got her nowhere. "So it's okay for a man to lie and cheat on his wife? You men figure as long as the bills are being paid and a roof is kept over their heads and there is enough money in the bank and enough room on the credit cards, he can do whatever he pleases?" Lita flipped her hand at Justin. "You're just stupid like the rest of them."

Justin rubbed his hand under his chin. "You don't understand, Lita. It doesn't mean that a man doesn't love his wife if he cheats. He lies to spare her feelings. Most of the time the man doesn't care about the woman he is cheating with." Justin looked down at his folded hands and then looked back at Lita.

"Don't you think I know that? I was on the receiving end, always am. Leonard didn't care about me. How do you think I felt walking into that big house after sneaking off for lunch, going to be with him, having him throw a couple of hundreds at me, and sending me back off to work." Lita didn't like the way Justin was looking at her. She was wondering what was on his mind. "I figured he should have done a whole lot more for me for what I was giving him. He used me and he got what he deserved."

"He used you? You used him, Lita. Leonard was not your husband," Justin said. "How could you be so cruel to Myra? How could you let her know you were sleeping with her husband? You ruined both their lives."

Lita was almost speechless. Justin was defending a cheating, lying man. She wondered if he realized what he was saying. He was blaming her for the breakup of Leonard's marriage. "What do you mean that I was cruel by letting her know that I was sleeping with her husband? You are a jackass like all the other men I know. Just because he blames me for his wife finding out about our affair doesn't make me feel bad." Lita finished her rum and Coke. "Order me another drink."

"Are you asking me or telling me?" Before she could answer, Justin told the waitress to bring two rum and Cokes.

"Had it ever occurred to you that if Leonard had never cheated on his wife that I wouldn't have had anything to tell?" Lita asked.

Justin came right back at her. "And if you had never told her, they would still be together right now."

Lita took a couple of deep breaths. "So who's the victim, Justin?"

"Not you," he answered.

"Whether you jackasses want to believe it or not, Myra was the victim," she said.

"Victim, my ass." Justin took a sip of his drink. "And stop calling me a jackass. Do you know that Myra walked away with a small fortune? She is set for life." Justin slammed his glass on the table.

"Good, she ought to thank me. I made her a rich woman." Lita was thinking how she wished she were in Myra's shoes right now.

"Yeah, now she's a rich woman with no husband. You know how hard it is to find a good husband these days?" Justin asked.

"Justin, darling, it is not hard at all." Lita winked her eye at him. "It's impossible."

"A cheating man is not a bad man as long as he is not physically or mentally abusing his woman and is taking care of her every need," Justin said.

"What about emotional abuse? Lita asked. "So you are telling me it is all right for a man to have women on the side and a faithful wife at home?"

"There's no emotional abuse if she doesn't know about it," Justin said. "And yeah, that's every man's dream to have a faithful wife. Who wants a cheating wife?"

Lita was trying not to show the disgust and hatred toward men on her face. “Who wants a cheating man?”

“You do, Lita. As long as they have enough money, you do.”

Chapter 17

"Ma'am, do you have any idea who would want to do this to you?" The policeman slowly scribbled something in his notebook. He quickly took a couple of glimpses at Arlene. He was trying not to be so obvious in admiring her beauty and at the same time trying to control his lustful thoughts that he didn't want to enter his head. "Any jealous boyfriends? Girlfriends?" The policeman looked at her with raised eyebrows and waited for her to answer. "It goes both ways you know. Boyfriends get mad at girlfriends and girlfriends get mad at . . ." he cleared his throat, ". . . girlfriends. This looks like the work of a jealous ex." He took a deep breath and continued writing in his notebook. He took notice of the broken window on the front door, spray painted hedges and sidewalk with illegible graffiti. There was some unfamiliar black powder covering Arlene's white, wrought iron lawn furniture. Upon closer inspection, the police officer concluded it to be black pepper. "Pepper?" He wiped his hands on his pants after swiping some of it off of the patio table. He looked at Arlene. "Why the pepper?"

Arlene chained smoked as she paced back and forth through her foyer ignoring his insinuations. She didn't answer his question about the pepper. She figured the raised eyebrow look she gave him should have answered his questions that she had no idea why pepper was all over her furniture. She was wracking her brain trying to figure out who would do this to her. She didn't ask the question why. She had done so many men wrong and angered so many women that she knew something like this would happen sooner or later. She wasn't surprised. "No, I have no idea who would do something like this. I have no enemies," she lied.

"Ah come on, miss, everyone has at least one enemy. You mean to tell me you have gone through your whole life without making anyone mad?" The police officer focused more on Arlene than what he was writing in his notebook.

Arlene walked over and blew smoke to the right of his face. "Maybe. I have made plenty of people mad," she finally admitted. "But only crazy people do things like this and I don't associate with crazy people." Her hand was trembling. She tried to steady it so the cigarette would not fall from between her fingers. Her mind was telling her that her past had come back to haunt her. The cigarette fell from her hand and she didn't bother to pick it up. She clasped both sides of her head with her hands.

"Are you all right?" The officer picked up the cigarette and placed it on the patio table. The fire had gone out as soon as it hit the ground.

He escorted Arlene to the sofa to help her sit down. "Would you like a glass of water?" he asked.

"No. I'm fine. I suffer from migraines and the stress of this vandalism has set it off. I'll be okay." She walked into her living room and sat down on the oversized sofa. She leaned her back against the sofa pillow. "Do I need to answer any more questions?"

The officer closed his notepad and placed it in his shirt pocket. He stood there silently staring Arlene up and down. He couldn't help himself; she was gorgeous. "I think I have enough for now. Be sure and lock up, and don't hesitate to call me if you need anything else." He stood there for a moment before turning to leave. He was hoping that Arlene needed him to stay for a little while longer, even if it was just to vent about someone breaking into her home. He turned back around. "Are you sure you don't need me to stay a while longer?"

"Thank you, but I'll be all right." Arlene didn't like his glaring stare. She surely didn't enjoy looking at him. To her he was well below average. She looked over at the broken window pane on her front door. "No one can get in through that little window on my door that's broken?" she asked.

"Doesn't look like they wanted to break in, just wanted to scare you a little." He was still staring. "Like I said, be careful and call if you need me."

Arlene thanked him again as she slowly got up from her sofa and walked him to the door. She closed it and securely locked it. She pulled on the handle to make sure it would not open. She couldn't think of anyone who was that mad at her to damage her home and property. She now began to think it could be the work of a crazy person.

The broken glass was still on the floor next to the door. After she swept it up, she went to her bedroom to retire for the night. The ringing of her phone startled her. She didn't feel like talking to anyone, so she didn't answer. She figured her answering machine must have been full because it did not come on. The light was blinking, which meant she did have messages. She decided to wait until the morning and check them. The walk to her bathroom seemed to take forever. She was ready for a long, hot bubble bath before she went to bed. What she saw when she entered the bathroom stopped her dead in her tracks. Too scared to move, she stood there for a moment before she slowly backed out of the bathroom and reached for the cordless phone that was supposed to be on her nightstand. She couldn't find it. Panic and fear had overtaken her. Suddenly she remembered she laid it on the bed. She called the number on the card the officer gave her and told him he needed to come back.

*****

"I don't understand." Officer Henderson looked puzzled. "I checked the whole house when I was here earlier. Nothing else was out of place or out of the ordinary. The bathroom sure wasn't like this when I checked it. Who would write, Y*ou can't have him* on your bathroom mirror in lipstick? And who is the him they are referring to? Whoever did this is really upset at you for them to smash every glass container you have in here. Look at your candles. They are all broken." Officer

Henderson looked over at shaking Arlene. "Ma'am, I don't know what to tell you. Someone must have been hiding in here all along while we were downstairs. This is a big house. I guess that's why we didn't hear anything." He looked over to the curtain in her bedroom. "What's over there?"

Arlene turned around. "It's a door that leads out to my patio." She walked over to the door and pulled back the curtains. Everything was still in its place. The potted plants were still neatly arranged near the edge of the porch area.

Officer Henderson walked over to take a look. "There are no broken windows on this door, and it is still locked." He pulled on the door. It didn't open.

Arlene looked around her room. "But how did they get in?" Arlene asked.

"I wish I knew the answer to that." The officer scratched his head. "I hate to ask you this, but are you seeing someone's husband?"

"Of course not," Arlene snapped back. Carole and Lita quickly came to mind. They both were after Justin and so was she. They were the only ones who were in competition with her over him. "You know what officer, I think I will go stay at a hotel for now and come back tomorrow. I know I won't be able to sleep here tonight."

"I think that's a good idea," the officer said. He looked around one last time. "What the hell is going on here?" he mumbled.

"Could you just stay until I pack a few things?" Arlene went quickly to her closet and grabbed her overnight bag.

"Of course, not a problem," the officer said as he watched her walk from the closet to the dresser.

Arlene went through her drawers and closets as quickly as she could. She was more angry than scared. She was trying to figure out which of the women had done this to her. Carole came to her mind before Lita. She wasn't sure if Lita even knew about her, but she knew about Lita. She had checked Justin's answering machine from her house earlier in the day. She heard the message Lita left about being a little late for their get together at Dalveaux's. She quickly finished packing, thanked the officer for his patience, got in her car, and drove to the nearest Holiday Inn wondering if she should retaliate or not.

Chapter 18

"Are you Denise?" the doctor asked. He put his pen back in his coat pocket before reaching out to shake her hand.

"Yes I am." Denise extended her hand to greet the doctor. Her right hand was limp as she slowly raised it to meet his. She was worried about her friend. "How is Gina?"

"We're still running tests. She's in severe abdominal pain. She has told me that you know all about her condition." The doctor motioned for her to sit down on the sofa in the waiting room. He continued to stand.

"What can I do?" she said while fidgeting with her hands. She didn't know what to do with them. Finally, she rested them in her lap. "I don't know what I can do or what to say, Dr..." she paused because she didn't know his name.

He sat down beside her. "I apologize, I'm Dr. Greer. I'm still waiting on the test results before I can tell you what the next course of action will be."

Denise slid in the opposite direction away from the doctor. "No apology needed. I'm just concerned about Gina. Is she getting worse?"

Dr. Greer noticed how uncomfortable she became when he sat down so he stood back up. "That's a possibility. We're not sure. We should have the results in about an hour. If you want, you may go in and see her now."

"Thank you, Dr. Greer." She slowly stood up, picked up her purse, and held it close to her chest. All kinds of thoughts went through her mind as she walked down the hallway towards Gina's room. She turned around to thank Dr. Greer again, but all she saw was the back of him as he went in the opposite direction to see his next patient.

Denise slowly opened the door to Gina's room. "Hey, Gina," she whispered. Denise walked over to the bed and picked up Gina's hand and gently squeezed it. "Are you in much pain?"

"Yes," Gina whimpered. "It hurts so bad and I can't hold anything down."

"I'll just sit here with you. Don't try to talk, just relax," she said. Denise tried to make the queasy feeling in her stomach go away. Hospitals made her sick to her stomach. She let go of Gina's hand and dug in her purse for a peppermint. She found a piece of chewing gum and popped it in her mouth. She walked over to the sofa and sat on the edge of it. She didn't know what else to say. Her eyes became blurry and her skin was clammy and wet.

Gina looked around the room and noticed that Denise had come in alone. "Where's Nicole?"

Denise stood up and walked back over to Gina. She held Gina's hand again and squeezed it tighter this time. "She's at the movies with a couple of friends. I left a note telling her where I am."

Gina's face tightened from the pain. "About our discussion, I think it would be better not to tell her anything. Just let things stay the way they are." Gina looked at Denise for some sign of approval. "I've never been a mother to her and she hates me. I can tell by the way she looks at me."

"That's funny, she said the same thing about you," Denise said.

Gina smiled. "Really? I guess she gets her critical ways from me."

"Hold up girl, no one can top you." Denise leaned over and kissed Gina on the forehead.

"She's a good kid, but I'm just not mother material. It's probably a good thing that I didn't raise her, since I'm getting ready to dic."

Denise looked at her with misty eyes. "Stop talking like that. You would've made a great mother someday. You just weren't ready at the time."

"Timing has nothing to do with it. I've never wanted kids. I don't dislike them." She took a deep breath. "Promise me you'll make sure that she gets all of her checkups and necessary cancer screenings. I do have a heart. I don't want her to suffer with pain like I'm doing right now." Gina looked up at the ceiling. Her gaze was fixed. She was struggling with emotional guilt.

Denise clasped both of her hands around Gina's. "I need to ask you something." She watched as Gina continued to stare at the ceiling. "It's important, Gina."

"No Denise, I don't want her to know that she's my daughter."

"That's not what I'm talking about," Denise said. "I know all about your medical history, but nothing about her father's or who he is for that matter."

Gina stopped staring at the ceiling and tried to sit up. She managed to get halfway up. Denise helped her the rest of the way. "I don't know if that's a good idea, Gina. Does the father know about Nicole?"

Gina wouldn't answer. "I thought we agreed to never talk about who her father is. You promised me that when I let you become her guardian."

"Does he?" Denise asked again.

"Damn it," Gina yelled. "Yes, yes he knows, but he's just like I am. He wasn't ready for a child and he still isn't." Gina looked away from Denise. "We were both selfish and we still are. We only thought about ourselves. There was no room for a child in our lives."

Denise moved away from the bed. "It's Eddie, isn't it? You were too embarrassed to tell anyone because of his drug problem." Denise took a deep breath. She walked over to the wall near the television. It was on but the sound was turned down. She reached up and turned it off. It was a distraction even though there was no audio coming from it. "I need to know, Gina, just in case he may want her back when you are no longer around."

"Want her back. He never had her and didn't want her. Neither of us did. It was a blessing to Nicole that you were around because there is no telling where she would be today." She clutched the rail of the bed. The pain was becoming unbearable. "Where is that doctor?"

Denise could almost feel her pain. She walked back over to the bed and stroked Gina's head. "Rest my friend, maybe we can talk about this tomorrow." Denise couldn't get the image of crackhead Eddie coming into Nicole's life at this point out of her head. The girl was almost grown so maybe that was a good thing. He couldn't take her even if he wanted to.

Gina grabbed Denise's hand. "There may not be a tomorrow. I think this is the end. The pain is killing me."

"This is just a setback, I'm sure it's not time for you to leave us yet. You still have a lot of commotion to throw into people's lives." Denise was trying to ignore the fear on Gina's face. Every time Gina grimaced from pain, Denise tried not to display a look of shock or pity. She wanted to remain strong for Gina.

"I wish I could believe that. Like I told you, no one lives forever," Gina said.

"Have you told Eddie about your illness? Does he know?"

"Yes, I told him and he has been there for me. I know it may be out of pity. But I do need someone. Loneliness is not a good feeling." Gina closed her eyes until the pain passed.

"What did he say about Nicole?" Denise didn't want to know if she wanted to hear the answer or not.

"Nothing."

"Just as I thought. He's too busy living the fast life instead of trying at least to inquire about his daughter." Denise picked up her purse to leave. She needed to walk out for a while. She wanted to get some air. Gina wasn't giving her the answers she wanted to hear.

Gina saw Denise heading for the door. "Wait, Denise. Don't go yet." She covered her mouth as she coughed. "Please!"

"I'm not leaving the hospital. I just need to get some air." Denise took a couple of deep breaths. I'll be back. I won't leave until I make sure you're okay."

"You mean you want to make sure I'm not going to die tonight." Gina sat up straighter and reached for the cup of water on the stand. She picked it up and took one sip. "I'm scared, but I'm prepared to die. I have made peace with God and asked for forgiveness and I've accepted his will. I have no choice but to do that."

Denise quickly backed away from the hospital room door. "Excuse me." Dr. Greer walked in with the test results. Before he could speak again, a nurse followed behind him and gave him a message before he had a chance to inform Gina of her results. "Dr. Greer, Dr. Norris is on the phone for you. I was told to come and get you as soon as he called."

"Thank you," he said to the nurse. He turned to Gina. "I'll be right back. I have to take this call." He left hurriedly out the door and bumped into a young woman who was in the hallway crying. He asked if she was all right as he quickly rushed by her. He was in too much of a hurry to hear her answer. He told her he would send a nurse over to help her as he continued on his way.

As soon as the doctor left, Gina started trembling. She knew what he was about to say. She was glad that she had a little more time to prepare herself.

"Calm down, Gina. I'm here for you. We will get through this together." Denise managed to hold back her tears.

"How long did he say he would be gone?" Gina asked.

"Who?" Denise asked not paying attention to who Gina was referring to. Her mind was on a lot of other things.

"The doctor," Gina said.

Denise embraced Gina. "He didn't say."

"Promise me when I'm gone that you won't give Eddie a hard time. He really isn't a bad person. He just can't focus on one thing for too long. It's not his fault." Gina looked at Denise with pleading eyes.

Denise didn't want to argue with Gina. The bad news from the doctor would be enough for Gina to bear. "Okay, I'll lay off of him."

"You know that new sports bar that just opened up?" Gina grabbed a tissue out of the box from the stand next to her hospital bed and wiped a tear from her eye.

Denise pretended not to notice the tears streaming down Gina's face. "I've heard about it." She rubbed her weary eyes. "I've heard that it is very nice and that the inside has an upscale look to it."

"I gave Eddie the startup money to open it. He says he is going to pay me back." Gina leaned her head back on the pillow on her bed. "It's his sports bar."

"You really think he's going to pay you back?" Denise envisioned Eddie as a hustler, a swindler, or a con artist, not a businessman. "I'm sure he got his business sense from the streets."

Gina ignored her comment. "I also drew up a will and I left a trust fund for Nicole. I'm not as heartless as you think. It doesn't matter where you tell her it came from. She won't have access to it until she is eighteen."

"Don't you think that's a little young?" Denise asked. She started thinking about how Gina thought money would solve just about anything. That was all she talked about when they were in high school.

"Age is just a number, and you never know how long you're going to live. Look at me; I thought I would be here until my eighties." Gina turned on her side and faced the wall. She started crying. "It's not fair," she cried. "Why? What did I do to deserve this? Why did I have to be born if I was going to die so young?" Gina sat up on the edge of her bed and after a couple of moments of silence, started crying hysterically.

It had been two hours since Denise ran to get a nurse and two doctors to handle Gina. Denise assisted them in holding Gina down so a nurse could give her a sedative. Gina was now coming out of her sleep.

She slowly opened her eyes and looked over at the IV needle that was stuck in her right arm. "What happened?"

Denise walked to the table and poured Gina a cup of water. "Nothing, besides your usual drama." Denise smiled and handed the cup to Gina. "You put on quite a show, girl."

"Oh, now I remember," she said, coming out of her grogginess. "I thought I was fine with my illness. I guess I'm in denial." Gina looked at the IV in her arm again. "I wish I could have just died in my sleep."

Denise didn't say anything for a while. She changed the course of the conversation. "So, what did you leave Eddie? You kept calling his name while you were sleep. You kept saying that you left something for him."

"Nothing, just the money I gave him for his business." Gina started rubbing her arm. The medicine in the IV sent a burning sensation through her veins.

"So he won't have any claim on Nicole's money?" Denise sat down next to Gina. "I'm just trying to cover all bases. I don't want any surprises. He may just want to claim her when he finds out she has a trust fund."

"He won't." Gina looked down at her hands. She took her diamond ring off and handed it to Denise who reluctantly took it. "That's for you. I want you to have this."

Denise twisted the ring between her fingers. "You don't have to do this. I don't want you to think you have to give me anything." She held the ring tightly and after thinking about it for a few seconds decided to accept it for sentiments sake. "Thanks, I will cherish this. But I know you will be around a while to see me sport this bad baby."

"To answer your question about Eddie, he has been by my side when everyone else was putting me down. Sure he had a drug problem, but he is a kind man. I remember when I first told him I was pregnant with Nicole. He was in shock. I had always used protection when I was with him, so he couldn't understand how I got pregnant." Gina looked away from Denise. "He finally put two and two together and realized I had been cheating on him. He loved me so much that he agreed to go along and tell everyone that he was the father of my baby. I didn't want children so I declined his offer."

Denise had a stunned look on her face. "You mean Eddie is not her father?"

"No, he isn't. He tried to talk me into not giving her up when she was born. He even offered to marry me, but I was too selfish for him and my child." Gina could feel a calmness coming over her. Her heavy shoulders became light. "I guess I better hurry up and come clean before I take my last breath." Gina leaned back and closed her eyes. The intense pain was coming and going.

Denise got scared. Her heart started beating fast. "Gina, Gina." She touched her on the shoulder.

Gina opened her eyes slowly. The drugs still had an effect on her. "I'm still here girl, haven't gone anywhere yet." Gina felt like she had to vomit, but nothing would come up. She sat back up again. She felt better that way. "Promise me that you won't ever mention this to anyone or ever try to find her father."

"Wait. Does he know where Nicole is?"

"Yes." The pains were coming more frequently. "That doctor better come on. I'll be dead by the time he tells me I'm dying." Gina gripped the side railing of the bed until the pain that traveled through her body subsided.

Denise became nauseated at the sight of Gina being in pain, but maintained her composure. "You don't think he will come to get her?"

"That's the last thing you have to worry about. He hasn't done anything in seventeen years, why would he come now? He is too self-centered, like me, to let anything get in the way of his life." Denise leaned over the railing; sweat was streaming across her forehead. She didn't know how much time she had left. "Justin," she yelled. "Justin Vanderbilt is Nicole's father."

The cup of water Denise had in her hand fell to the floor. She stood there trying to swallow the lump in her throat. All kinds of thoughts went through her mind. *Justin has enough money to get whomever he wanted, including his child,* she thought.

"Oh. My. God." Denise quickly wiped away the tears that fell from her eyes as she saw the hospital room door slowly open.

Dr. Greer came in with a chart in his hand. "Sorry it took me so long to get back to you, Gina. I have good news and bad news," he said.

Denise walked over to Gina's bed, sat down, and embraced Gina. Her mind wasn't on the test results. She was thinking hard and fast about what to do if Justin wanted his daughter.

Gina figured the bad news was that she was going to die, and the good news was not today.

Dr. Greer sat on the foot of the bed and patted Gina on the leg. "Well, Gina, the bad news is that you have a bad case of food poisoning, the worse I've seen in a long time."

"Food poisoning," Denise said. "Food poisoning." she repeated.

Gina touched her stomach. "So you are telling me the food poisoning is making the cancer pain worse?"

Dr. Greer flipped through his chart. "No, what I am saying is that the food poisoning is what's causing your stomach pain and vomiting."

Denise moved closer to Dr. Greer to take a look at the chart as if she knew what she was looking at. She watched as he flipped through the pages. "How can you tell that her pain is not from her cancer?"

The doctor looked at Denise and smiled. "How do I know?" he asked. He looked over at Gina. "The good news is your cancer is in remission. You will be going home soon. Not today, but soon," he said. He sat the chart down on the end of Gina's bed. "A nurse will be in here soon to take your vital signs again. I will check on you again later." He looked over at Denise, extended his hand to shake hers. "It was nice meeting you."

"Same here," she said as she took her hand from his.

Dr. Greer was happy to give the good news. "I'm sure you two have a lot to discuss and plans to make." He turned to exit the room and then turned back around. "Does anyone know who that young lady was who was standing by the door? I saw her take off in tears down the hall as I entered the room."

"No," they both said.

Denise walked outside the door and saw roses strewn everywhere.

Nicole had been there and they didn't even know it. She saw the message her mother left when she got home. She had one of her friends drive her to the florist to get roses for Gina. She felt bad for her, but after everything she heard outside the door, she didn't care if Gina lived or died.

*****

"Where do you want me to tow it to?" The wrecker driver took off his gloves and handed Carole the clipboard of papers for her signature.

"Take it to the dealership on 610 and South Main." Carole had her hands clasped behind her neck. "I don't know who could have done something like this." Carole looked around and saw a couple of boys standing in the corner of the building near where she had parked. She wanted to ask them if they damaged her vehicle or saw who did, but she decided against it. "I will just get another one tomorrow," she told the driver. Carole's vehicle had never been vandalized the three years that she has parked it behind her shop.

The driver gave her a wide-eyed look. "You mean you're not going to get it fixed? All you need are four new tires, a new back window, and new belts. Somebody must really be mad at you. They didn't even try to steal it. Have you called the police?"

"For what?" she asked. "What are they going to do?"

"I guess you're right. It's not like they are going to go door to door and ask questions. They will probably tell you that you are lucky that it's not stolen." The wrecker driver tore Carole's receipt from his book and handed it to her.

“That damn Lita. I know she is behind this,” she said under her breath. Carole was glad that she fired her, but she knew Lita was right about finding competent help. She had to admit that Lita was good at what she did, at the boutique that is. She was thinking about selling the boutique, but not until she found a man who could cover all of her expenses and more.

“Can I drop you off somewhere?” The wrecker driver finished hooking the Escalade to his tow truck.

It hadn’t crossed Carole’s mind that she did not have a way home. “No, I will call someone.” She got her cell phone and called one of her men who she knew would get out of bed, tell his wife some lie, and be there in twenty-five minutes to take her home.

Chapter 19

Lita had skills. If I had not known she was a hater and she had been truthful, she could have gotten anything she wanted from me. But instead she is a lying, manipulative gold-digger. Justin was thinking about their night together and how freaky Lita was when she was under the influence of alcohol. He lost count of how many drinks she had consumed after the third one. They ended up together at his place to have sex after leaving Dalveaux's.

Their little hideaway where he and Blair used to hang out when they wanted to get away from it all was just about ten miles ahead. Justin had not been there in about six months. He had been so busy romancing other women that his grief for Blair had been put on the back burner. In his worst nightmare he never thought that she would die. At worst Blair would leave him. But death is something you can't beat.

He just wanted to hurry up and get to their *getaway* house. He needed to get Lita, Carole, and Arlene out of his head. He knew they were out to take him for what he had and love had nothing to do with it.

Walking into the house without Blair made Justin's heart sink to the pit of his stomach. He had never come here alone and had never brought any other women here. There was a blue silk scarf lying across the sofa. It still had the smell of Blair's perfume. He held it to his nose and inhaled deeply. The scent lingered in his nostrils. He walked into the bedroom. Dust covered the dresser where some of her jewelry lay. The closet was still filled with designer clothes, shoes, coats, and belts. *I can't take this. Why didn't I just ram my car into the guardrail? This pain is too much. I've got to be dreaming. Please let this be a dream.* Justin closed his eyes as he stood in the closet. The room felt like it was spinning. He just knew he was dreaming and would wake up any second from this nightmare. After sitting in the corner of the closet crying and talking to himself for thirty minutes, Justin walked back into the living room and decided to take a nap on the sofa, but not before making a couple of phone calls.

*****

Dalveaux's Sports Bar was jumping. It was jammed packed every night. Eddie sat back and enjoyed the scene. He was relaxed and poised. It seemed as if all eyes were on him. He rubbed his hand under his freshly shaven chin. His hands were smooth and soft, much different from the days when his body was drug infested. Eddie liked his new chiseled body. He was glad that his crack days were over. He had been clean for a year. The twenty-five thousand dollars that Gina had lent him to open the bar was in his bank account ready to be repaid to her. She was one of four investors that lent him money for his business. He felt good that he was able to pay her back and everyone else. The sports bar was a hit.

"Hey, Eddie man, what's going on?" Leonard walked in like a bolt of lightning. Being chased and hated on had taught him how to walk past women at the speed of light.

Eddie turned around and saw Leonard whip around the corner. "What's up, Leonard? You shot out of here the other night so fast that I didn't get a chance to say hello." Eddie stood up and shook Leonard's hand. "Was that Justin Vanderbilt you were with last time?"

"Yeah, man," he said, looking around for familiar faces. "We go way back. He's a good friend of mine."

Eddie motioned for Leonard to sit down. "What can I get you to drink?"

"Bud Lite," he said.

Eddie caught the waitress as she walked by. "Candace, sweetie, two Bud Lites." Eddie took out a cigarette and lit it.

Candace blew him a kiss. "Sure thing, sweetie."

Leonard slowly looked around the bar. The last person he wanted to see was Lita. He didn't want to be caught up in her trap again. She had a way with men. "Dalveaux's Sport's Bar. Where did you get that name from?" Leonard asked.

Eddie looked at the flashing sign behind the bar. "It's my mother's maiden name. Didn't want to use Franks. Franks Sports Bar or Eddie Franks Sports Bar didn't have a good ring to it."

"Dalveaux's is good." Leonard looked at all the women swarming around the men. Sports were the last thing on their minds. This was a gold-diggers paradise. "You should have named this mug Haters and Chasers club. The only things the men are watching in here are the women."

Eddie surveyed the scene. Not one eye was on any of the big screen televisions. It was more like a club atmosphere. Men were dishing out cash and collecting phone numbers faster than the blink of an eye. "Haters and Chasers club, you might have something there, Leonard. These women are seriously working the room."

Leonard let out a big chuckle. "Check this out. Friday nights should be your haters night and Saturday nights should be your chasers night. Get in free before ten o'clock."

"There is not a charge to get into this sports bar. They get in free," Eddie said.

Leonard made eye contact with a couple of women, and then quickly looked away. "Club, man, turn it into a club. Do you know how many fool men would flock to this place just because it is filled with women, gold-diggers or not? Women don't care anymore if people know they are haters or chasers."

Eddie had a serious look on his face.

Leonard saw Eddie's look of uncertainty. "Hey, man, I was just kidding with you. Your business is booming. Leave it like it is. I was just having fun." Leonard glanced over to one of the televisions to see what was on. Two women were blocking his view and smiling. They raised their glasses to him and he returned the gesture. "Well, Eddie, I am glad to see that you're doing well, but I'm out of here."

"You're always running in and out. Stay a while man and chill." Eddie saw the women trying to mark Leonard as their territory.

"I got to keep running. I've been caught before and I'll be damned if it happens again. There are too many women in here who take their jobs seriously." He drank the last of his beer and slammed the bottle on the table. The two women were still eyeing him. "I won't be hated or chased anymore." He stood up, straightened his jacket, gave the women an "I am out of here" salute, told Eddie goodbye, and double-timed out the bar.

Chapter 20

Gina was on cloud nine and happy to be home. She was still feeling a little queasy from the food poisoning. The mushrooms she had in her salad two nights ago must have been bad. Hearing the doctor tell her that her cancer was in remission was the best thing to happen to her in a long time.

"Do you need anything before I go?" Denise put the last of Gina's things in her bedroom. She made sure all of Gina's dishes were washed and that she didn't need any food before she left

Gina let out a sigh of relief. "I have all I need. Come here. Let me give you a hug." She reached for Denise and held her tight.

"I'm always here for you, girl." Denise was so glad that Gina's attitude had changed. Maybe the cancer scare had adjusted her attitude. She wished that Gina would stop competing with everyone. "I would stay longer, but I need to get home. Nicole must not be feeling well.

She was still in bed when I left."

"Oh, I was wondering why she wasn't with you." Gina walked to the office area of her home and started going through her file cabinets.

"She gets in her little moods sometimes. I just try to stay out of her way until it passes."

Gina found what she was looking for and walked to her sofa to sit down. "I can relate to that." Her eyes quickly scanned the documents. She flipped the pages then went back to the beginning and read it again.

"I'm so glad that things turned out well for you. You're looking great. What do you plan on doing now?" Denise started gathering her things as Gina continued to look through her papers. She was so glad that Gina was more tolerable and generous than before.

"I have some bills I need to catch up on. My bedroom is a mess. I have clothes thrown everywhere." Gina was still going on and on about what she needed to do while she read over the papers she had gotten out of her files.

"Maybe Nicole and I will come back later if she is feeling better." Denise was glad that her friend was showing her human and caring side.

Gina looked up from the papers she was reading. "Thanks. I could use some company later on. I rested enough while I was in the hospital." Gina flipped through the papers one last time, folded them, and placed them back in the envelope. "Oh, first thing Monday morning, I'm going to my lawyer and redo my will." She looked at Denise without batting an eye. "I won't be leaving anything for Nicole since I will be around for a while. It's a good thing she didn't even know about it."

"Okay," Denise said stiffly. Her forehead became heavy. She felt her shoulders slump, but the only thing on her arm was her purse. Gina's words burdened her. She was so upset that she couldn't stay in the same room with Gina any longer. After what Gina just said, Denise didn't know if she could remain friends with her. She left and slammed the door behind her.

Gina opened the door before Denise could make it to the car. "If you come back this evening or whenever, bring my diamond ring back that I gave you."

Chapter 21

The banging on the door awakened Justin. He sat up on the couch and looked around to familiarize himself with where he was. He got up and peeked out the window. Carole was propped against the porch pillar. Justin stood with his hand on the doorknob, debating on whether to open the door or not, thinking it might be a mistake to let her in. He decided he would. He opened the door quickly. "You found me," he said with a grin.

"Of course. Do you think I am some kind of idiot?" Carole asked.

Justin looked at the unfamiliar vehicle in the driveway. "Where is your Escalade?"

She didn't tell him it had been vandalized. "Oh, I got tired of a truck. I decided it was time for me to drive a car instead. Do you like my Lexus?" She brushed quickly past him and entered the house.

"Nice," he said.

"Thank you." She looked back at the driveway. "Where is your

Jag?"

"In the garage. Would you like a drink?" Justin closed the door and walked to the bar.

"No, I'm fine." Carole watched him pour a drink for himself in an ice filled glass. "So, what did you call me over for? I know it wasn't just to talk." Carole walked toward the bedroom and peeked inside. "Nice place. How long have you had it?"

Justin noticed how she was sizing up his pad. He knew that all she was interested in was material things. "About three years," he said. He watched her go into the bedroom, quickly survey it, and slowly waltz out.

"Kind of dusty in here." Carole ran her hand across the dining room table as she walked back towards Justin.

"I know. I haven't been here in a while." He gulped down his drink, walked back to the bar, and refilled his glass.

Carole walked over to Justin and took the glass from his hand, took a sip, and placed it on the bar. She pulled him in close to her and ran her hand up his back. "Let's get down to business. I can't stay long." Carole moved her hand from his back to the front of his stomach, up to the middle of his chest, caressing it.

"Why can't you stay long?" he asked.

Carole quickly ran her tongue across Justin's lips. "I'm working on opening up another boutique and there is a lot of paperwork that I need to finish." She laid her head on his chest not wanting to let on that her real next business venture was him. "Would you like to invest in my new business?"

"Maybe," he said.

She took his hand and started to lead him to the bedroom. "Let's talk about it later."

Justin let her hand go as soon as he heard a knock on the door. "Excuse me." He picked up his glass and took a quick swallow, running his hands across his head.

"Whoever it is, get rid of them," she demanded. Carole took a deep, disappointing breath.

Who does she think she's talking to? he thought. Justin walked to the door and looked out the peephole. A smile came to his face. *Damn. This is going to be good.* He opened the door and there stood Lita.

Carole's face turned red. Her eyes were bucked. She walked over and stood close to Justin as if she were laying claim to him.

Lita looked at Justin with questioning eyes. "What's going on, Justin?" Lita slammed the door behind her as she walked in. "What the hell is she doing here?"

"Ladies, ladies, calm down. There's enough of me to go around." Justin burst into a drunken laughter. The two bourbons that he quickly swallowed had him on a high. He walked over to his favorite leather chair and sat down. With feet propped on the coffee table, Justin looked the women up and down wondering how they came to be like they were, women with no shame or morals. Never mind that he was a dog.

"Okay, Justin, I know I'm kind of wild and all, but if you are thinking about the three of us together you can forget it. I hope that's not what you called me over here for." Lita had the most evil looking expression on her face.

Carole became angry. "Oh, so you called her too. Well it's not that kind of party."

Suddenly the door swung open. It was Arlene. She was pulling into the driveway when she saw Lita go through the front door. She thought she was going to make a surprise entrance. Justin was the only one who was not startled.

Justin was slumped in his chair with a dreamy look in his eyes. "Arlene, I see you finally made it. What took you so long?"

Arlene was speechless only for a couple of seconds. "What are they doing here?" She walked over to Justin and sat on the arm of the chair. She stroked his head gently. "Are you all right?" She kissed Justin on the forehead thinking it would make the others jealous.

Justin looked at her with a big grin on his face. "Cut the crap, Arlene. You're not going to be on my payroll." She jumped up and tried to slap Justin across the face, but he was too quick. He caught her arm in midair. "You have one more time to attack me, just one more. If you do, I promise you that I am going to put my foot as far up your ass as I can get it."

She yanked her hand from Justin's grip.

Carole started to leave. She had more men than she could handle right now. She would see Justin some other time.

"Wait, wait, wait, wait," Justin slurred. "Where do you think you are going?" He motioned for Carole to come back.

"I'm leaving. I don't want to be around these psycho women. I don't need you Justin nor do I want your money," she lied.

"Now, why do you want to call them psycho? And who said anything about you wanting money?" He paused and motioned for her to close the door. "What have they ever done to you?"

Carole closed the door. "I can't prove anything, but a lot of strange things have been happening to me and I know one or both of them are up to it."

"Strange things like what?" Lita asked. "Are you trying to accuse me of something because I have no idea what you're talking about. I have better things to do than to be concerned about your life."

"You tell me." Carole sat down on the sofa and crossed her arms and legs, waiting for an answer.

Lita leaned against the fireplace mantle. "I haven't done a thing to you."

"You wouldn't admit it if you had."

"I don't have time to play games with you, Carole," Lita hissed.

Arlene moved away from Justin. "Let's stop the bull right here and now. Somebody is playing games, dangerous games, and it's not funny."

Justin was back at the bar pouring himself another drink. "What are you so upset about, Arlene?"

"Let's just say something happened the other night and it really upset me." She looked at Carole and Lita like they knew what she was talking about.

"What happened?" Justin asked.

"Nothing. I don't want you to worry. I can handle it."

"Worry, I don't worry about anything anymore. I don't give a damn about anything anymore. My whole world is gone. There is nothing here for me. You three bitches made sure of that." Justin was slurring his words as he spoke.

All three of them looked as if they wanted to band together and kick Justin's ass.

"Did you say bitch?" Carole asked.

"B-I-T-C-H," he spelled. "Bitch, yes that's what I said."

Carole got close to Justin's face. She pointed her fingers toward Arlene and Lita. "You see that over there? Those are bitches. Anyone who is gutless enough to go behind someone's back and damage property and scheme to get what they want is no good. Don't put me in the category with those things standing over there."

Justin took Carole by the shoulders and walked her over to Lita and Arlene and positioned her next to them. "Now you are one of them."

Arlene moved away. "You're drunk. You know that? I have never seen you act like this before."

Justin waved his arm. "Nooo, get on back over there. Let me look at you three." Justin leaned back in the chair and propped his feet on the coffee table. "Gold-digger number one." He pointed to Arlene. "Are you a hater or a chaser?"

"I don't know what you're talking about, Justin." Arlene moved away from the other two women.

He looked at the other two. "Carole, Lita, hater or chaser?"

No one wanted to answer. They just stood there looking at one another.

Arlene walked over to Justin and sat on the arm of the chair again. "Justin, baby, slow down on the drinking." She bent over to whisper in his ear. "Let them go on about their business."

Justin kissed her on her lips and was about to run his fingers through her hair when she caught his hand and held it.

"Still don't want that hair messed up," he griped.

Carole shook her head. "It's probably a weave and she doesn't want you to feel the tracks in her head."

Arlene quickly moved away from Justin before he got a chance to see if Carole was telling the truth.

"Have a seat everyone." Justin motioned for them to sit on the sofa.

They declined.

Carole headed for the door. "I've got better things to do than stand here and listen to your rambling."

"Going to check on your truck?" Justin swirled the ice around in his glass.

Carole turned around. "What did you say?"

"Why did you go and buy a Lexus? It won't cost much to get your truck fixed."

"How do you know about my truck?" Carole put her hands to her chest. Justin never came to mind when she was trying to figure out who the destructive culprit was. "It was you?" she asked in a pitiful tone.

Justin didn't answer. He just pulled a large blade out of his pocket, the one he used to cut the belts and puncture the tires on Carole's truck. He turned to Arlene. "Arlene, Arlene. I thought sure you were going to make a play for that policeman. He sure had eyes for you."

"What policeman?" she asked.

"Oh come on, sweetheart, don't play games with me. You're not good at them. No warm candle lit baths for you for a while. That bathroom was a mess; broken candles everywhere and bubble bath spilled all over the floor."

"You were in my house?" She was stunned. Cool, calm, Justin was the one who destroyed her peace of mind.

"Hey, you told me I could come and go as I pleased."

Arlene had given Justin a key to her house and told him he could use it anytime, night or day.

"I was on your bedroom patio the whole time. That policeman never checked outside your patio bedroom door. You forgot that your key fits your bedroom patio door too and thanks for giving me the code to your house alarm. When he went back downstairs, I came back in." Justin was now past the drunken stage.

Arlene was too startled to say anything. She hadn't taken anything from Justin. Why did he vandalize her home? She couldn't come up with a good reason. Surely he couldn't be mad about the small attack she launched on him when he literally called her a prostitute.

"Lita," he said. "You like to go creeping down people's neighborhoods at night. I was looking out of my window the night you called and saw you rolling past my house."

"You put the note on my car when it was parked outside the boutique." Lita became infuriated. "What kind of man are you to scare someone like that? So what if I passed by your house. It's no crime and it didn't hurt you."

"Okay, Justin," Arlene said. "I can only speak for myself. Yes, I was trying to play you for what you had. That's no reason for you to be that upset with me. You had the option of telling me that you didn't want to see me again. I would have eventually left you alone if I couldn't have had you all to myself." She held her hand up. "I'm a chaser. I was trying to get the commitment along with the money and security."

The other two confessed to nothing. They both kept their mouths shut.

Justin walked to his desk drawer and pulled out the envelope. He handed the pictures to Arlene, the tape to Lita, and the earring to Carole. He stood in front of the door, blocked it with his body, and forcefully ordered them to sit down. Frightened, they all obliged. Justin took out the letter Blair had written. He unfolded the paper and stared at it for what seemed like an eternity. He looked at the women with intense hatred on his face. He started reading.

"Damn, lying ass, Justin,

What have I done to deserve this? I loved you so much that I couldn't see past your lies until now. I have been there for you through thick and thin. I believed every word that you told me. You had me believing that all my suspicions of you being unfaithful were in my head. You thought that your money and power could overshadow your infidelity and keep me close to you. It is clear to me that you don't know what true love is and my love wasn't enough to bring you home at night. You didn't even love me enough to let me go. Instead you conditioned me to believe your lies. I have been everything to you that a man wants in a woman, but that wasn't enough. Perhaps Lita, Arlene, and Carole can give you what you want. I suppose there was something in each of these women that you could not find in me. I thought you were the one for me, but I guess you are the one for all of the women who will have you, since you think there is enough of you to go around. They can all have you now. I hope you find what you are looking for since I didn't have what you needed.

Goodbye, and I mean GOODBYE! FOREVER."

Justin folded the letter and laid it on the table. All three women sat there speechless, waiting for someone else to say something. He thought about how much Blair had meant to him, but he was too busy running all over town, instead of showing Blair that she was one of the most important things in the world to him. His worst fear was Blair actually catching him with another woman. He never imagined she would die. He wished he could turn back the hands of time. He realized that it is true that you never know what you've got until it's gone.

Lita threw the tape on the table. "What's this? Why are you giving me this tape?"

Arlene and Carole were caught. Arlene was in the pictures she sent Blair, and the earring Carole had left in Justin's bed was custom made. Carole was the only one around with earrings like that. Blair had commented on how unique they were when she and Justin were in Carole's shop one day.

"I listened to the tape, Lita. You did a good job of not saying much at all. No one can even tell it is you. But I made a stupid mistake. I guess you were so into it that you didn't realize that I called your name three times. I got to admit, you really put it on me." Justin poured himself another drink. He didn't want his buzz to wear off. "There is nothing more for me to do. I sure as hell don't want any of you. So stop with the games. It was good while it lasted. All three of you are murderers. It's as if you had taken the gun and shot her yourself. None of you can compare to Blair. Why would I want some scheming, conniving woman?"

Lita wasn't about to fall for that one. "I want to hear the tape." She had a look of hope on her face. "Justin, you told me you never call out women's names when you are in the heat of the moment. Anyway, that is not me on that tape," she lied.

Justin had called her name on the tape, and since she wanted proof, he went to the desk to see if he could find the mini-cassette recorder. For once he had slipped up and called out a name. "Just to let you know I'm telling the truth, I will play it for you, if the others don't object. Then I want all of you to get the hell out of my house."

Arlene was sitting quietly twirling her hair around her finger. Lita was on Justin's heel as he went from his desk to the kitchen looking for his recorder. Carole was pouring drink after drink to calm her nerves.

Justin couldn't find his mini-cassette recorder. Then he remembered he had put it in the garage. "I'll be back." The thought of leaving the women together in the room made him think twice. "What the hell," he mumbled. "If they fight, then let it be. I don't give a damn." He went into the garage to get the recorder.

Arlene got up from the sofa and moved to the chair. "So, you say it's not you on the tape?"

"Why don't you just go home, Arlene?" Lita looked at Carole. "You, too."

No one wanted to be the first to leave. Justin was in no condition to be left alone. Someone had to stay and keep him company.

Carole slid to the other end of the sofa. "What makes you think you get to stay?"

"Because I'm not like you two." Lita was hurling insults left and right at Carole and Arlene. She looked over at the table and saw the tape that Justin left. Lita picked it up and was about to pull it loose.

"No, you don't, Missy." Carole walked up behind her and grabbed the tape. "I know what you are thinking. I would have done the same thing, but you are out of luck. We are going to listen to this tape."

Lita tried to grab it, but Carole drew her hand back quickly. She looked toward the door. Justin was taking a long time. It sounded as if he was throwing things off the shelves.

Carole put the tape down her blouse and sat back on her end of the sofa. "I don't think you are bold enough to come and get it." She stuck out her chest like she dared her to try.

"Don't get your hopes up. I knew there was something a little funny about you. Trust me, my hands will go nowhere near you."

Carole gave her a sly little smile and patted her breast. "I'll just keep the tape here for safe-keeping until Justin gets back."

After ten minutes of arguing, Arlene eased herself away from the women and walked to the kitchen door that led to the small, one car garage to see what was taking Justin so long. She heard sounds of tools falling off the wall onto the concrete garage floor. There was a continuous humming noise coming from inside, then the loud sound of a car door slamming shut made her jump. Her hand was on the door knob. She gripped it tightly and slowly turned the knob and pushed slightly. When she opened the door, fumes came rushing in. The fumes she gulped in as she inhaled made her cough. She stepped back. "Justin, Justin, where are you?"

Carole and Lita rushed to the door. They could hear the low humming sound in the garage. Arlene had a platter in her hand trying to fan the smoke out of the kitchen. She threw the platter to the floor and the three of them ran into the garage to find Justin. The white smoke blinded them as they approached the door of his car.

Justin was sitting in his Jaguar with the motor running. He was just sitting there barely awake in the driver's seat.

Arlene opened the car door. Justin was coughing and gasping for air. "What is wrong with you? Come on, get out," she screamed. "Help me somebody."

Justin pushed her away as she tried to pull him from the car. "Get away from me." He tried to close the door but the seatbelt buckle that was hanging out of the door kept it from shutting.

Lita and Carole both pulled Justin from the front seat while Arlene held the door open. Once he was out of the car Arlene closed the door and helped them prop Justin against the car so they could help him get his balance. They helped him stumbled his way to the kitchen door.

Lita tried to open the door to turn the ignition off, but one of them accidentally hit the lock when they took Justin out. Carole ran to the passenger's door to see if it would open, while Arlene pushed Justin into the kitchen. On her way out she saw that they could not get the doors open, so grabbed a hammer off the garage wall.

Justin stood in doorway clearing his lungs. "Where are you going with that hammer?"

"Close the door and get back in. You have inhaled too much carbon monoxide to be out here. Your doors are locked and we need to break the windows to turn the ignition off." Arlene closed her eyes and took a whack at the driver side window. Nothing happened.

"No, don't break my windows."

Arlene, being the protector she was, pushed him further back. "Do you have an extra set of keys?"

"Not with me. They are at home."

"Hurry up," Lita yelled. "Hit it again!"

Arlene ran to the car and started banging on the windows. Still nothing happened.

"Hit harder," the women yelled.

Justin watched as they banged and banged and banged. He remembered he had custom glass that was hard to break. Suddenly he didn't care about the window or car anymore. He wanted to die and they came and rescued him. He didn't care what happened to him anymore. He couldn't get the image of Blair out of his head. He just wanted to die. Those three women out there banging on his car had killed him just as they did Blair. The combination of alcohol and carbon monoxide was starting to get to him. He could barely keep his eyes open, but he knew there wasn't enough in his body to kill him, at least not that night. He could hear the women still banging on his car window. He blamed them for messing up his life. They rescued him, but he swore he would not give them another chance to cross paths with him again. He closed the kitchen door, locked it, and went over to the sofa to lie down. He didn't care about anyone or anything anymore.

He could hear Lita, Carole, and Arlene beating on the kitchen door for him to open up. They were screaming harder and beating louder every second. Justin didn't care. There was no way they could leave the garage. The automatic opener was in his car and Justin knew they would see the damaged switch on the wall he had yanked out earlier when he was in a rage. Coughing, gasping, and beating, that's all he heard. The more he heard it, the better it sounded to him. He walked to the bar and poured himself a drink. He sipped slowly and listened to the sounds of death coming from his garage. He guessed that by this time tomorrow they all would be resting in peace, including himself. He was going to check out too. He just didn't know how he would do it. He got tired of hearing the screams coming from the garage. They hadn't stopped yet. He walked over and turned on the stereo. Just be a man about it, by Toni Braxton was playing. He wondered if Blair would still be alive if he had admitted his infidelities, asked for forgiveness, and done the right thing. He knew if it really came down to it that he could admit that he had been unfaithful and he knew that Blair would forgive him. What he didn't know is if he could actually be faithful to one woman. He knew Blair was the kind of woman that he had wanted as a wife, but he just wasn't sure if he could be faithful. The song was beginning to depress him, so he turned off the stereo.

His glass was empty. As he walked to the bar, he noticed the screams had stopped. He listened for about two hours just to make sure all was quiet. Not a sound was heard. He knew the deed was done. He figured there were three fewer gold-diggers that men had to deal with. He reached the bar, poured another drink, and raised his glass in the air to propose a toast. "Carole, Arlene, and Lita, rest in peace, cause you sure caused a lot of hell here on earth. This one is for you, Blair."

Chapter 22

Denise hadn't heard from Lita all morning. She realized that she must not care about her personal belongings that were still at the job. She figured Lita must have found Mr. Rich after all. She just hoped Carole didn't call or come waltzing in asking about why Lita's things were still there. She was hoping not to hear from either one of them. Denise could feel the frustration of her simple life about to overtake her. She was getting tired of the same routine day after day. She prayed that something better would come along.

*****

The day went by quickly. The boutique had been busy as usual. Denise was just glad to be home. She guessed that Nicole must have been feeling better since she had cleaned the kitchen and cooked dinner. She was even speaking to her in a civil tone. Denise picked up the remote and flipped through the channels. Nothing good was on.

She wondered what Lita was up to because she had not heard from her all day. Carole hadn't called or come by either. It wasn't unusual for Carole not to come by the shop or call. She was the boss. Some days she called and some days she didn't.

"Hey, Mom." Nicole came out of the bathroom while combing out her hair.

Denise almost jumped off the couch. She was the splitting image of Gina. For a moment she thought Gina had just walked out of her bathroom. Nicole had dyed her hair the same color as Gina's. She never realized how much they favored. "What have you done to your hair?"

"I dyed it."

Denise kept her composure. Nicole was almost eighteen, a good kid with good grades and had never been in trouble. Getting upset with her for dyeing her hair should be her least concern. There were far worse things that Nicole could be into. She walked over and inspected it more closely. She was hoping it was a wig and Nicole was playing a trick on her. "It will take some getting used to. What made you choose this color?"

"I don't know. I just did." Nicole walked to the hallway mirror to take another look. "Gina called for you. She says she has been trying to reach you all day."

Denise had been avoiding Gina's calls. She thought back to the last time she talked to her. She had phoned Gina as soon as she returned home that day, hoping that Gina had changed her mind about taking Nicole out of her will. Gina told her she didn't see any need for Nicole to know the truth about her. Denise told her fine, it was her call, and that she would bring her diamond ring back to her. Denise didn't want to face Gina, so she sent it by courier instead. Gina came back from her thoughts after Nicole repeated again that Gina had called. "Thanks, I will call her later," she lied. Denise knew she never wanted to talk to Gina again. Ever.

Nicole sat on her bed. She wondered if she should tell Denise that she knew the truth about who her mother is. She didn't want to hurt Denise, the one who took care of her when her own mother didn't want her. She hated her father and mother. She hated the fact that she had two rich parents who knew about her and couldn't care less what happened in her life.

Chapter 23

Justin had ridden his motorcycle back to town. The wind blowing in his face made him feel free. He was on a natural high. His drunkenness had worn off hours earlier. Riding off into another world seemed like a good idea to him. All his money and possessions didn't mean anything anymore. His woman was dead and now he was a murderer. He knew what happened the night before. He let three women die in his garage in the country. He didn't care if he got caught. He had been living a meaningless life. He wanted to go out with a bang. Tonight he was going to party until he couldn't party anymore. His adrenaline had him pumped.

An hour and a half later, Justin was back at his home in the city. The marble floors of his entryway looked cold. His house was not a home. It was a shelter; a place to store his clothes and furniture. He didn't feel welcome in it anymore. He hadn't really felt anything since the day Blair died. He closed his eyes hard, hoping when he opened them again, he would wake up from this nightmare. He was still standing in the entryway on the cold marble floor in his bare feet. He didn't remember when he took his shoes off. He opened his eyes, nothing had changed. He knew then that his life at this moment was real. Reality had finally sunk in. He decided to shower and go out on the town. He called Leonard and talked him into meeting him at Dalveaux's later on that night.

Justin and Leonard met outside on the sidewalk of Dalveaux's Sports Bar. Justin was looking good in his gray Versace suit. He was clean shaven and the scent of his Cool Water cologne filled the night air. His right wrist was adorned with a Rolex watch. That way everybody noticed it. Justin could hear the music from the sports bar playing. The music, the beat kept haunting him. Blair loved coming to the bar to listen to the loud music. It almost brought him to a breaking point, but he knew he couldn't have a breakdown in public. He didn't want to go out like that.

Leonard had an uneasy look on his face as they stepped into Dalveaux's. The mood was upbeat and festive, but the noise level was lower than usual. People were laughing, drinking, and getting to know one another better. This night, the men out-numbered the women almost two to one, but the haters and chasers still represented well. "Man, why did we have to come here? This place is bad news, too many vultures in here."

Justin slapped Leonard on the back. He was glad the song had finished playing by the time they got inside. It brought back too many memories. Memories that he no longer wanted. "Don't be such a wimp. Come on in here. What are you scared of? Lita?"

"Why did you have to go and bring her name up?" Leonard quickly turned around to see if she might be sneaking up on him from behind.

Justin took a deep breath. "Well, I can assure you she won't be here."

Leonard surveyed the place. He wanted to get his life back on track. "Two drinks is my limit. I want to be sober when shovels come out. There will be no digging in my pockets, especially from the women in here."

"Live, man. You only have one life. This moment, right now is all you have. Live today like there is no tomorrow." Justin rubbed his hands together while scoping the crowd.

Leonard pushed Justin's hands down. "How many drinks did you have before you got here? You are talking like you can foresee the future, rubbing your hands together like you're a fortune teller."

"I can, man, I can." He thought about how he wanted to spend his last night before he left for good. Wine and women, what a way to go. *They finally got the best of me, brought me down to my lowest. I let go of the one that had me lifted and got involved with three who didn't give a damn. After tonight, we will all be resting in peace.* Justin came out of his thinking mode and looked around for a seat at the bar.

Leonard ran to the nearest table. Justin was moving too slow for him. He wanted to get in and out in a hurry. He took a seat and ordered a drink from the first waitress he saw.

Justin bypassed the bar and joined Leonard at the table.

"What took you so long, man? You know you are prime rib in this town and so am I by association. I don't need this drama from these broads up in here." Leonard was nervously tapping his left foot to the beat of the music.

Justin saw how Leonard's foot was moving to the music. "Hey man, why the foot work?"

"I guess I'm nervous seeing all the single women in this bar. They are only here for one reason." Justin was still standing. He wasn't ready to take a seat. He was enjoying the view. "Gold-diggers are like drugs. You know they are not good for you, but you just can't stay away. You always tell yourself you can stop at any time. They should have a rehab place for men like us who just can't stay away. That just say no stuff doesn't work."

"I have been rehabilitated. Myra made damn sure of that after she found out about Lita and me. She won't give me the time of day. She really took me to the cleaners." All Leonard could see was wall-to-wall women. "I'm just as broke as these diggers up in here. I will be back on my feet in a couple of months. But I'll be damned if I give my hard-earned money away again. I know how to say no and spell it to them if they don't understand the word."

Justin was staring at a woman who had just come out of the restroom. "Blair," he mumbled. He knew he was drunk, but he knew Blair when he saw her. Her hair was shorter, but that face, that shape was etched in his mind.

Leonard turned around and looked toward the bathroom. "Hey man, you've had a little too much to drink. She does favor Blair, but man that's not her."

Justin finally sat down. "Yeah man, just tripping. She is about the third woman that I've seen in the last couple of months that looks like Blair."

The woman saw Justin when he was looking at her with his mouth wide open. She took that as the opportunity to approach him.

Leonard saw her making a beeline for the table. "Damn, here she comes. I think I'm going to get my drink and move."

"She's coming over here for me, not for you, just sit tight." Justin had a big grin on his face as she approached. Damn, she looks almost as good as Blair. All of a sudden, a reason for living brought him back to life. Gold-digger or not, I can work with that.

She extended her hand when she reached the table. "Hello, my name is Tracy."

Justin stood up. "I'm Justin Vanderbilt." He turned toward Leonard. "This is my friend, Leonard Cavanaugh."

"It's nice to meet you, Leonard."

Leonard stood, shook her hand, and sat back down. He was still analyzing her. She seemed a little different from the other women in the bar. She acted like she actually had brains. He especially liked her because the second sentence from her mouth wasn't asking for a drink.

"So what brings you in here tonight?" Justin moved his chair closer to her. He was feeling rejuvenated.

Tracy pointed to the giggly women in the corner. "They did. Those are my old high school classmates. I'm in town for our 10-year class reunion. I had to move away from them because they were getting a little loud. My girls have definitely changed. They were so smart in school. Now all they want to do is party all the time."

"They look like they are in Lush City." Leonard looked at how wild they were acting. He looked over at Tracy and saw that Justin couldn't take his eyes off of her. "Where do you live now?"

"Jackson, Mississippi," she said.

"What made you leave Houston for Jackson?" Leonard asked.

"That's where my mother is now. She owns a bed and breakfast and I help her run it." She pulled out a business card and handed it to Leonard. She looked at Justin who was just mesmerized. "What's the matter? Is there something wrong with my face?"

"No, not at all. You just look like someone I know."

"Well, I don't think we have met anywhere, because I would have remembered you." She took out another business card and gave it to Justin. "What are you two drinking?"

Leonard almost choked. "You buying?"

"Of course. You have a problem with that?" she asked jokingly.

"No problem at all. I will have about three Crown on the rocks," Leonard said.

Justin chuckled. "You decided to go big time, huh? I thought two drinks were your limit?"

Tracy winked at Justin. "That's okay, women get men to buy drinks they can't afford. It's all right. I got it covered."

"Thank you, sister," Leonard said. "And by the way, I can afford more than two drinks." He laughed.

They partied until two in the morning. Even Leonard loosened up a little and held a conversation with a woman. She even bought him a couple of drinks. He realized that all the women weren't in there for the same reason. He knew Justin felt he had hit pay dirt with Tracy. She was smart, attractive, and had a job.

Eddie sent a round of drinks to Leonard's table. He congratulated him for not running out and for staying in a room full of women for more than fifteen minutes. "Are you all right, man?"

Leonard looked at him with a grin on his face. "Yes, I'm all right and I intend on staying that way. Thanks for the drinks, but you can take them to another table. I have had my limit. I don't want to get too comfortable or vulnerable in here."

"I hear you, man." Eddie saw Justin and Tracy all cozy at another table. "It looks like Justin had a good night."

Leonard looked at his watch. "And it looks like he may have a good morning also."

"I think you are right," Eddie said.

Leonard finished his drink, thanked the nice woman he was with for a pleasant evening, and left like he had come—alone. He knew that Tracy and Justin had something else in mind once they left the sports bar, so he didn't bother to say goodbye to them. He would catch

Justin another time to get the details. They acted as if they had always known each other, so he figured Justin was in good hands.

*****

It was 2:45 a.m. Justin slid the key card into the door. His buzz had almost worn off. He had stopped drinking around 11:30. He figured he and Tracy would end up together somewhere, and he wanted to be sober. He couldn't believe that yesterday he thought about ending his life. He still didn't know how he would explain how three women ended up dead at his house in the country. He decided to think about that later. Besides he knew he had enough money to buy his way out of anything. He wanted to enjoy his night with Tracy.

Tracy plopped down on the king-sized bed. "I am so glad to be sitting still. I have been on the go all day."

Justin sat next to her and laid her on the bed. He took her shoes off and started rubbing her feet. "Don't get tired on me now. This is only the beginning." He started massaging her calves and moved his hands up her thighs.

"Oh, baby, I will give you a night that you will never forget. I know a lot of women have probably told you that, but I deliver what I promise." She took his hand and stopped him before he could go any farther.

"Don't scare me yet, let me go shower first." Justin got up and went to the bathroom. He looked like a kid who had been let loose in a candy store.

Tracy stood up to get undressed and blew him a kiss. "If you are scared, call 911."

"Oh no, I like being scared with what you got."

They both had showered and were standing on the balcony of the hotel. Justin was standing behind Tracy with his arms wrapped around her.

"This is so romantic." She pushed herself closer to Justin.

"You are so beautiful, Blair," he whispered.

He realized what he said. He just stood there hoping Tracy didn't realize what had just come out of his mouth.

Tracy heard, but didn't say anything. She didn't want to spoil the mood. She didn't owe him anything and neither did he. She just wanted to enjoy the moment. It had been a long time since she had been with a man. She had been so consumed with her work that she couldn't find time for the little pleasures in life.

Justin took her hand and led her to the bed. They both slipped off their robes and slipped under the covers. "You feel so soft." Justin kissed her on the neck, then behind her ear. He let his tongue travel her body from head to toe, then back again. She liked it so much that he did it again and again until she begged him to stop.

Tracy rolled Justin over and straddled him. She pleasured him until he was almost unconscious.

All Justin could think about was Blair. He didn't want to open his eyes until they were finished. He wanted the fantasy to last as long as he did, which wasn't long, because Tracy suddenly killed the mood.

"Who is Blair?"

"Huh, what?" Justin was confused. "Where did that come from? Why are you asking me about another woman in the middle of sex?" He started to wonder if he had called out Blair's name again.

"You called me Blair earlier. Is that you wife?"

Justin rose up. "Wife? What makes you think I have a wife?"

"I don't think we would be in a hotel if you were single."

Justin lifted Tracy off him and sat up. "Well, I figured since we just met, that you would feel safer in a hotel. I could have been a murderer or something, and no I'm not married."

"Or maybe you thought I was. Or maybe you thought I had some other plan in mind and you didn't want me knowing where you lived. Is this what you rich guys do?"

"Who said I was rich?"

"Come on, Justin. Everybody in town knows about you."

"You're right. Everybody in town who has been here for the last seven years knows about me. If you left ten years ago, how do you know so much?" Justin waited for an answer. "I should have listened to Leonard. You all know every trick in the book. That was a good game you ran." Justin pushed the covers off him and put his robe back on. "I bet you went somewhere and had fake business cards made."

Tracy sat up and brought her knees to her chest with a pillow on top of them. "I made them on my computer."

"A pretty face and sexy body, that's all you women have to work with. What happened to your minds? You make it bad for a good woman to have a chance with a man, because we are too busy wondering if you are out for money instead of love."

"You wouldn't know what to do with a good woman if you had one. What makes you think you deserve a good, faithful woman? I heard that you sling dick all over town."

Justin picked up his wallet, took out two one hundred dollar bills, and laid them on the dresser. "When I find a good woman, I will do what a man does when he finds one."

"You no good son of a bitch. What are you going to do with a good woman? Will you do her like you did Blair? Will you come around when you think she is about to leave you and throw money at her to make her stay? Just because you throw a lot of cash at your woman and don't take care of her other needs, do you think that she won't let another man have a tap at it? You got lucky with Blair. No matter how much you dogged her out, she couldn't bring herself to sleep with anyone else. She got offers. But I guess you want to know how I know so much, you no good son-of-a-bitch."

A haunting feeling came over Justin. Those words sounded so familiar. He turned toward Tracy with the angriest look in his eyes. He started to rush to the bed, but his feet would not move.

Tracy was kneeling on the bed tying up her robe. "Yeah, Mr. Can't Keep It Zipped. It's me." Tracy yanked the short-haired wig off her head. Her long wavy hair fell down to her back.

It can't be. Justin's heart was pounding.

"Didn't I tell you," she said, waving a gun that she had in her robe pocket, "if I ever saw you again that I was going to kill you. Didn't recognize me, huh?"

Justin realized it was Janice, Blair's sister, who was eighty pounds lighter, toned, and trim, wearing a short wig. "Wait a minute Janice, hold on. Wait a minute."

"Hold on to what? Wait for what? Is that what you told Blair? I watched her hold on, wait on, and cry for you. I have always hated you for what you put her through. Now she is gone because of you."

Justin took two steps toward Janice. He was now actually scared of dying. His overindulgence in women had caught up with him. He was going to die by the hands of a woman who was upset because of his infidelity. He would rather be killed by a jealous girlfriend. He would have felt better if it were Blair standing there ready to pull the trigger. He finally realized that Lita, Carole, and Arlene were not to blame for Blair's death. He was the one who was lying, cheating, and sexing every woman he could get his hands on.

"Say your prayers because it's lights out for you." Janice covered the barrel with the pillow and shot Justin three times.

Justin saw his whole life flash before his eyes in rapid motion. Visions of how he treated Blair and how he never spent time with the daughter he had. Blair sitting by the fireplace with a short satin nightgown. Nicole in the boutique with Denise while he is shopping with Blair. Crying, tears falling from Blair's eyes while she is standing in his living room while another woman is in his house. Spying on little Nicole swinging at the park. Blair on his back as he walks through the park. A picture of Nicole on Denise's key chain on the counter at the boutique. Blair crying again, because he's lying again. Blair, Nicole, Blair, Nicole. Lover, daughter, lover, daughter. His joys, pains, and death were at the mercy of women he had crossed paths with. The visions passed slowly away. Then there was darkness. Justin closed his eyes, never to open them to this world again.

*****

The maid found Justin's body at ten that morning. Janice was long gone. She changed her clothes when she left with her hair flowing down her back. As far as she was concerned, Tracy never existed. Justin was the only one who really knew who she was. She even lied about knowing the women at the sport's bar. She saw a group of women, pointed them out to Justin and Leonard, and then took it from there.

Lita, Arlene, and Carole were found the night before. The garage caught on fire and the firemen found their bodies. The police had been looking for Justin all that night, but he never made it home. They now knew he was dead also.

Chapter 24

Denise was worn out and still in a state of shock. In the last six months, five people she knew had died. She had gone to all the funerals except Arlene, whom she didn't know that well. She just knew her from her visits to the boutique, which wasn't that often. No one was clear on who killed the three women or Justin. The investigation was still ongoing. All that anyone knew about Justin was that he left the sports bar with a woman named Tracy, whom the police were still looking for in Mississippi.

Nicole walked over to her mother and gave her a hug. She held on tight. She couldn't bear the thought of losing her. She couldn't imagine going through life without Denise. "Are you all right?"

"Yes, I'm fine." She stroked Nicole's honey blonde dyed hair and laughed quietly to herself. *You may look like Gina, but you take after me.*

"What are you going to do, Mom?"

"About what?"

"A job. The boutique is closing down in two weeks if it isn't sold to a new owner."

Denise didn't want to think about that right now, but she knew she had to have a plan. Since Carole was dead, one of the investors was trying to buy the boutique and have Denise run it.

"I can get a job to help out." Nicole rose up and looked at her mom. "I'm old enough now. You have struggled to take care of me, now I want to help."

"We'll see. Let's not talk about it right now." Denise knew it was about time for her to loosen her reins on Nicole. The phone rang.

"I'll get it." Nicole ran to answer the phone. "Hello."

"Ms. Delaney," said the voice on the other end.

"This is Nicole."

"Is there a Denise Delaney there? This is Dr. Greer. I am Gina Frost's doctor."

Nicole's knees weakened. "Mom, it's Dr. Greer."

"Gina. Is it about Gina?" Denise walked to the phone with her hand on her chest.

"I don't know, he didn't say."

Denise took the phone. "Hello, Doctor."

Denise was answering yes, then no, then yes again. She finally thanked the doctor for calling and hung up.

"What did he say?" Nicole asked.

"He wanted to know if I had heard from Gina. She left my number as a contact number. No one seems to know where she is." Denise was not really worried. Gina was probably off in another country somewhere vacationing. She would often disappear months at a time and then suddenly re-appear bragging about her travels and showing off her expensive items she had purchased.

Chapter 25

It was finally here. Nicole was celebrating her eighteenth birthday. Gina was nowhere around. Nicole didn't care, as long as Denise was by her side.

"Happy Birthday, baby." Denise kissed her on the cheek.

Daniel, Denise's brother who was visiting from D.C., walked in slowly from the kitchen with Nicole's birthday cake. "Where do you plan on going to school?"

Nicole was counting the candles on her cake. "Just making sure all of them are there. I'm thinking about Texas Southern University. I just don't know what I want to major in yet." She didn't want to go to college out of state and leave Denise alone. She was accepted at Spelman, which is where she had her heart set on going. She promised to help her mother out and that's what she was going to do. Her father was dead and they hadn't heard from Gina in months. She must still be out somewhere in the Caribbean. That's the message she left two months ago. "Thanks for the cake and the watch." She hugged Denise and Daniel and took her bowl of ice cream and cake into her room.

"You raised a really good child, Denise." Daniel sat on the sofa next to her. "Whatever she decides to do, I know she will be good at it."

She patted Daniel's hand. "Thanks, I just wish I could have done more for her. Now that she is grown she spends her time worrying about me."

"I worry about you too, Denise. Why won't you let me help you until you get back on your feet?"

"I'm doing fine, Daniel. If I need anything, I promise I will let you know."

"No you won't." He sighed. "You're just like Momma. She would smile to the end and say everything was all right when it wasn't. She didn't want any man throwing in her face what he had done for her. You have that same attitude." Daniel leaned his head back on the sofa. "I love you, Denise. You're my sister and I want to help."

"If I need anything," she said with emphasis, "I will let you know. Stop worrying about me." She sat up. "I love you too, brother."

"I am going to the kitchen to get cake. Would you like a piece?"

"Yes, just a small piece."

Hours later, there was a hard knocking on the door. "It sounds like someone is knocking on your door." Daniel walked to the door to see if anyone was there. He looked out the peephole. "Hmm, must be your man. Denise there is someone at the door dressed like he just stepped out of a magazine."

Denise didn't know who it could be. "Open the door and see who it is."

Daniel swung open the door. "May I help you?"

"Is Denise Delaney here?" The man's powerful voice almost intimidated Daniel, but he kept his composure and didn't let it show on his face.

"May I ask who you are?" He tried to make his voice sound just as deep.

He held out his hand. "I'm Jack Hamilton. I'm an attorney representing the late Justin Vanderbilt."

Denise tripped over an ottoman trying to get to the door. She wondered what Justin's attorney wanted. A gripping fear came over her. She figured Gina had something to do with this, that's why no one had heard from her in months. "What's this all about? Did Gina send you?"

Jack raised his hand and reached in his blazer pocket. "Miss Delaney, I know nothing about this Gina you are referring to. I am here on behalf of the late Mr. Vanderbilt." He handed her a thick envelope. "Call my secretary to make an appointment to finalize everything after you have read the paperwork. Goodbye and you two have a nice evening. By the way, tell Nicole happy birthday."

Denise stared at the envelope for a long time before she opened it. Her hands were shaking and her eyes were filled with tears. She read the contents slowly and silently. A burning heat came over her body as the tears were now streaming down her face.

Daniel caught her as she fell to her knees. "What is it? What does it say?"

Denise couldn't say anything. She handed the papers to Daniel. He read them and could barely catch his breath. "Oh my God. What does this mean?" He read it again just to make sure he understood the contents clearly. "Oh God, I wonder if Nicole can handle this?"

Nicole was standing in the doorway. She heard and saw everything. She was too shocked to move. "What was my father's attorney doing here?"

Denise was stunned that Nicole knew about Justin. Denise's brother and mother knew the truth about Nicole. She never kept that a secret from them.

Nicole sat on the floor next to Denise who had not moved. "You were the only one who wanted me. You took care of me when no one else would. I wish I never knew the truth. But I am strong. I can deal with it. I just want you to be all right." She laid her head on Denise's shoulder. "I heard everything the day I came to the hospital to visit Gina. Gina can never have me. She will never be my mother. I don't care what those papers say. I am eighteen now. I can do whatever I want to do." She looked up at Denise and laid her head back on her shoulder. "Well, almost anything. You are still my mother and I am still living under your roof," she said jokingly. "I am all right because I have you."

She patted Nicole's shoulder. "I know there's a time for me to let go. I have held on to you too tightly." She looked up and smiled at Nicole. "And you know what? Pack your bags because you are going to Spelman."

"For a minute there, I thought you were going to say you were giving me back and we can't afford Spelman." Nicole leaned her back against the wall. "I will only go if you find a good job so you won't be struggling."

Denise took the papers from Daniel. She handed them to Nicole. "According to these papers, you can go wherever you want."

It had been a couple of hours since Denise handed Nicole the documents to read. Nicole opened the papers slowly. She couldn't believe her eyes. She did the same thing as Daniel. She read it over just to make sure she understood what the papers said. The words just about took her breath away. Justin Vanderbilt had left everything to his sole heir, Nicole Delaney. All she could think about was how hard Denise had struggled to raise someone else's child. She raised a child who was the seed of two people who were fortunate enough to help, but chose not to. She was not sad that Justin was dead, at least not today, but she was truly grateful for the money. She was glad that she had it for Denise. "Forget the job, Mom. I know I can take care of you now. And I am going to college, but I still don't know if I want to leave you here. You have done so much for me."

Daniel leaned over and hugged Nicole and Denise. "You deserve it after everything you and your mom have endured. Your mom will be all right. I will see to that. You had your heart set on going to Spelman, so that is where your little butt is going. I know I'm not your father, but let me give you some college advice," he said. "One, don't party too much, two, you have to study even when you don't want to, three, never let them know how much you are worth. And most importantly, watch out for those haters and chasers. Men do it too!"

Haters and Chasers
Men Do It Too

2014

www.ingramcontent.com/pod-product-compliance
Lightning Source LLC
LaVergne TN
LVHW091050080826
845145LV00002B/698